SHADOWS IN THE FOREST

Jennifer J. Morgan

Books by Jennifer J. Morgan

Libby Madsen Cozy Mysteries

Shadows in the Forest
Spa Shadows (summer 2022)
Shadowed Treasures (summer 2022)
Shadow Retreats (fall/winter 2022)
The Christmas Fairy - a holiday novella

SHADOWS
IN THE
FOREST

Libby Madsen Cozy Mysteries, Book 1

Jennifer J. Morgan

Secret Staircase Books

Shadows in the Forest
Published by Secret Staircase Books, an imprint of
Columbine Publishing Group, LLC
PO Box 416, Angel Fire, NM 87710

Book layout and design by Secret Staircase Books
First trade paperback edition: July, 2022

First e-book edition: July, 2022
* * *

Publisher's Cataloging-in-Publication Data

Morgan, Jennifer J.
Shadows in the Forest / by Jennifer J. Morgan.
p. cm.
ISBN 978-1649140890 (paperback)
ISBN 978-1649140906 (e-book)

1. Libby Madsen (Fictitious character). 2. Arizona—Fiction. 3.
Amateur sleuths—Fiction. 4. Women sleuths—Fiction.
I. Title

Libby Madsen Cozy Mystery Series : Book 1.
Morgan, Jennifer J., Libby Madsen cozy mysteries.

BISAC : FICTION / Mystery & Detective.

813/.54

To all the strong women in my family. My daughter forges her own path and lives life boldly, she's the kindest person I know and always inspires me to be my best self. My mother, my inspiration—to be creative, write, and live life to its fullest. My grandmother—her courage, her generosity, her devotion to her faith and loved ones, her love for exploring new places—it's clear where the rest of us get it from. And my two four-legged kiddos, Libby and Bella—I feel so blessed!

Acknowledgments:
To say that publishing my first book is completely unnerving, but also nearly the most courageous thing I've ever done, would be an understatement. Thank you so much to my publishers and editors! Thank you, Connie Shelton—so happy you enjoyed and I'm so appreciative of my first review! Also, to the beta readers who catch the stuff that many other eyes miss along the way: Marcia, Sandra, Susan, Paula, Isobel—Thank you! My family was so patient with me while I hid away to write … I'm so grateful to you for the freedom to follow my passion.

CHAPTER ONE

Right this way, please," I guided our newest client through the reception doors and into the women's locker room. "Once you've checked in at the front desk, you can leave your belongings in one of these." In my best Vanna White imitation, I swept my right hand out and around in an arc, selling the beautiful bamboo guest lockers. "Right here, you just punch in a four-digit code you'll remember. Make sure to leave your cell phone in your locker, and preferably turn it completely off. There are no cell phones allowed anywhere else in the building and for privacy's sake, please, no photographs in the locker room."

I paused as our newest client, Sasha, took everything in. Looking to her left there were two shower stalls and beyond those, two separate toilet stalls as well. The long white marble countertop, with several soft-lighted mirrors expanding the twenty-foot length of the room, provided space for clients to freshen up.

"You've thought of everything here, haven't you?" Sasha said as she looked through the various glass containers that held items such as Q-tips, ponytail holders, make-up remover pads, and then a variety of brands of leave-in conditioner, gel, lotion, and hairspray in a basket sitting in the middle of the countertop.

"We try to make it as convenient as possible, especially for our clients who leave straight from here to get back to work. All products are vegan and we make every attempt at locally sourcing most of our products. You'll find hair dryers, curling and flat irons, here in this basket." I leaned over slightly to pull out the wicker basket from the first shelf to our left just below the countertop. "There are fresh towels here and clean robes hanging there on the hooks. And this tall basket at the far end is where you will dispose of your used towels and robes." I demonstrated by lifting the wicker basket lid up and exposing the inside of the empty laundry bin.

"Wow, I'm so impressed! The lighting is so warm and comforting, too." Her eyes wandered toward the ceiling, observing the soft rose light coming from the space between the crown molding and the ceiling. The perimeter of the mirrors was also lit with a warm glow giving off the perfect amount of light. "How are you ensuring everything is disinfected between customers? You know, with the virus going around, that would be a concern of mine."

"Thank you for asking! We are padding the schedule so there's plenty of time between clients, which is why you see that you're the only one here right now—it's all yours! That gives us time between appointments to disinfect everything. And, as a spa business, we always inspect regularly for cleanliness—that's only become stricter recently."

"That's fantastic!"

"Here, let's continue and I'll show you the rest…we've barely touched the surface," I said proudly as I led her through the frosted glass doors with the Dharma Inspired Day Spa logo at the far end of the locker room. "Wait until you see our *Serenity Tea Room*."

Opening the glass door, we crossed the threshold into a darker space and took a moment to let our eyes adjust to even softer light. Soft wind chime music was audible, but not overpowering.

"Ok, now … wow! This is such an inviting space…" Sasha let her eyes roam over the entire room. There were love seats, reclining chairs, oversized pillow seating, as well as a full sofa at the other end of the room, all were upholstered in warm earth tones. The walls were a soft gray color with wall hangings showing various nature scenes, as well as stenciled inspirational sayings, and one beautifully painted lotus flower front and center on the wall. This was in the same shades of purple and gray as the logos found on all the doors. She walked immediately to the center of the room. "*This* has got to be the most beautiful fountain I have ever seen!"

"Ah, yes … this is made of healing crystals." The gently flowing water cascaded down a graduated set of crystals— five feet at the highest and down to about two feet for the smallest crystal pillar, the whole feature about seven feet in diameter. The crystals glowed softly in shades of rich blues, greens, and white.

"Once you're finished in the locker room, find a comfortable spot in here. Help yourself to our selection of teas—before and/or after your treatment. We always encourage our clients to allow time before and after your appointment time. You'll want to relax and enjoy yourself whenever you can. When it's time for your appointment, your therapist will meet you here and lead you to your therapy room."

"I may *never* leave … you make it so inviting," she exclaimed as she ventured over to the countertop where there were several heated carafes of hot water, a variety of mugs, all next to a wide assortment of herbal teas. "I've never seen so many varieties of tea! Lavender, rose, chamomile, as well as turmeric chai latte, spiced apple, and well, just way too many to choose from!"

"Well, we hope you enjoy. Let me give you the rest of the tour and then I'll leave you to relax before your appointment time. It looks like you will still have twenty minutes."

"There's more?"

I led her through the next set of frosted glass doors, continuing further to the back of the building. We walked into another decently sized space with doors along each of the three walls…to the right, the left and directly in front of us. "The massage rooms you'll notice are numbered 1, 2, and 3 and so on. One and two are to your left over there. Number three on the right side is our couple's room so it's a little larger. Straight ahead are an employees-only office and our laundry room. So, there you have it… now let's get back to the locker room so you can get ready for your session."

I ran into Alexis in the reception area as I stepped

through the doorway. Stunning as always, she was wearing her mauve-colored yoga pants along with a beautiful cream tunic with a pattern of bright flowers that accentuated her beautiful creamy mocha complexion. "Did I see you giving a tour?" she asked.

"Yep. New client, your neighbor, Sasha Adams. After her, I have Maggie coming in later and then I'm off to the mountains again."

"Maggie ... she's the quirky one, isn't she?" Alexis almost whispered. We were the only ones in the room, but I could see where it would be bad form if someone caught us talking about our bread and butter. "No matter, we're so blessed we still have new clients each week ... so thankful!"

"Indeed. Well, off to get my room ready. Enjoy your day!" I said over my shoulder as I was passing through the glass doors and on my way to the massage rooms.

Sasha was waiting in the Serenity Tea Room gazing at the fountain from her cozy spot on the loveseat.

I whispered to her as I neared, approaching from her right side, "Ready, Sasha?"

"Oh! I didn't even hear you approach. This fountain is mesmerizing!" She stood and followed me into the therapy room.

After I clarified a few things from her intake form and we discussed the particulars of what was bothering her today, I stepped out of the room to let her get settled on the table.

I stood there admiring our achievement once again, something I found myself doing often. My name is Libby Madsen. My business partner, Alexis Johnson, and I opened our day spa nearly two years ago. We met during massage school in our late twenties where we became fast friends and bonded over our love of healing. We both had other jobs at that time—Alexis dived right in to corporate life as an accountant right after college; I wandered around between multiple jobs…receptionist, store clerk, dog walker, you name it, I earned money doing it. Once we were both licensed as massage therapists, our dream was to one day open a spa of our own. It took us almost ten years to realize our dream, but here we are, the very proud owners of *Dharma Inspired Day Spa*.

I quietly knocked on Sasha's door. "Sasha, are you ready for me?" I heard a muffled *ready* and I walked through the door.

She was face down on the table, as we discussed, and covered in the privacy sheet. The next ninety minutes passed quickly. Sasha relaxed right into the massage and only spoke up to answer me regarding the amount of pressure and whether she was comfortable. Some clients are quiet and introspective during their sessions, others talk my ears off. Sasha was one of the quiet ones, I realized after our time together passed so quickly.

I spoke gently, "Sasha, your session is over now. I'm going to step out of the room. You take your time getting up, stretch a little, and I'll meet you right outside the door here with some water."

A few minutes later, the door opened and a sleepy-eyed Sasha appeared. "How are you feeling, dear?" I asked.

"Mmm … I'm so relaxed, I feel great! Maybe a little foggy-headed?" she answered.

"That's very normal. Here's some water; you want to drink a *lot* of water today to help flush all the toxins out of your body. I did some pretty deep work so you may be a little sore tomorrow. Take it easy, drink water, and get rest."

After handing her the water, we started walking toward the Serenity Tea Room.

"As I mentioned before, if you have time, you should sit and relax with some tea." I handed her a nice detox blend. "I recommend this one, and I'd really like to see you again within two weeks or so, if possible. You can schedule at reception on the way out, or later on our app, if you prefer."

I left her in the sanctuary drinking her tea and I went back to strip the linens in the room and get them in the laundry. I had one hour before my next session.

CHAPTER TWO

It is always so interesting to me that clients want to divulge so much about themselves while they are on my table. What is it about getting a massage that makes a person think I want to know every intimate detail of their life? Some days, I feel like I'm the priest in a confessional and I just listen and give the obligatory "uh, huh…," or, "go on…". Other days, I completely tune them out and plan the next adventure I'm going on. I've perfected my ability to act interested when I'm really not.

Recently back from an amazing trek, I could still see the gorgeous desert terrain of southern Utah where my sweet girl, Shadow, and I had hiked around near Arches National Monument. We spent two weeks camping and hanging out in the desolate, but eclectic towns of Moab and Kanab and seeing the most beautiful deserts—the gorgeous contrasts of reds, browns, and golden hues of the landscape are stunning. The billions of stars in the night sky were utterly breathtaking. Then, nearby, we also spent time in the mountains surrounding Bryce Canyon and Zion. Ah, to be back there now. *I should have taken more pictures.*

"Don't you think I have reason to be concerned?" the muffled voice broke through my lovely vision. *Oh, crap … I did it again.* Client on table. Maggie Crenshaw. Something about her daughter. Missing?

"I'm sure she'll turn up. You know how young ones are. She's having fun with friends and will call you soon, I'm sure," I said, really hoping I didn't give away how much I'd tuned her out. "Ok, Maggie, it's time to turn over." I held up the privacy sheet as she groaned, getting herself rolled over onto her back.

"Time sure seems to pass quickly every time I'm here … I can't believe we're halfway done already. I could stay here all day," Maggie said in that dream-like way.

Well, it's not like I can respond and tell her that she talks non-stop so no wonder the time passes quickly. No, I stayed quiet and continued to drape the sheet back over her and maneuvered it to expose her left leg. Applying a bit more lotion, I continued to gently work through her hamstrings in long strokes with light pressure. This client, unlike most of mine, preferred a relaxed massage versus deeper tissue work.

"When was Isobel expected home?" I asked.

"Two days ago. She's always been great about calling me if she is going to be late. This is so unlike her."

"Did you try calling her?"

"Yes, many times. Keeps going to voice messaging."

"I'm sure she's fine. Where was she going camping?"
See, I was listening.

"The Mogollon Rim."

"Oh, I go up there all the time. Which campground were they going to?"

Maggie thought about that for a second. "Something about a forest road number. Um, 171 maybe? I wrote it down at home."

"Oh. Hey, I know right where that is. I've stayed near there. It's an area with a ton of dispersed camping, without named campgrounds."

"Dispersed? What?" Maggie asked.

"It means that it's not really an organized campground that charges you to stay there. It's first come, first serve. Some of them might have a camp host, others don't."

"That sounds like a place they'd stay. They don't have any money to spend on campgrounds."

"Who did she go with?"

"A few friends from work."

"Where does she work?"

"Quality Computer in Tempe."

Man, her calf was really tight today. I wish she would allow me to go deeper into the muscle and loosen it up a bit. After doing what I could, I covered that leg and shuffled the sheet around to reveal her right leg and continued. She got fairly quiet, *finally*!

Working her quads, with a gentle motion in and around her knee and then a long stroke down to the ankle, I could feel her relax even more. As I finished up her toes on her right foot, my entire body suddenly got flushed so warm I imagined what a woman in menopause might experience. I was sweating. This was odd, why was I suddenly so warm?

It's not uncommon for a client to feel hot or cold during a massage, but why me? *I better not be getting sick. We are so booked right now; I can't take time off.*

Just then, I saw something flash before my eyes— almost like a vision. A blonde girl holding a leaf. There was a lightheadedness like I've never experienced and my heart was racing now. I stepped away from Maggie suddenly. Before I could even blink, it went away … no more dizziness, the heat in my cheeks went away, and my heart rate was getting back to normal.

"What's wrong?" she asked.

Taking a deep breath, I was trying to make sense of this. *What on earth was wrong with me today?*

"Sorry, I didn't mean to startle you, Maggie. Just needed a sip of water."

I covered her right leg and stepped around to the top of the table where I started working on her neck and shoulders. Tense here too.

"Tell me more about your daughter and this camping trip."

"Oh, I worry so about that girl. Sure, she loves the outdoors, but I don't think her friends realize that she's really a sick girl and can't be sleeping outdoors for nights on end."

"She's sick?" I asked.

"Well, she has asthma and she's diabetic, so of course I worry."

"How old is she?"

"Weren't you listening? I told you earlier. She's twenty." *And just when I thought I'd gotten away with that!*

"Yes, you're right, you did mention that. When I was twenty, I was always off on adventures and didn't see my parents for months on end. Of course, I didn't live with them. Wait, does she live with you?"

"Yep, mama's girl, through and through; can't get her to move out yet," she said so proudly.

"Hey, as I said, I'm sure she's fine, but I am heading up to the mountains for a couple days this week. I'll be right in that area and I would be happy to do some nosing around. See if I can catch up with her to let her know she needs to call her mama. How does that sound? Would that make you feel better?"

"Are you sure? You'd do that for me? I would feel much better if she had an extra inhaler with her."

"Well, sure. I'm there anyway ... no problem. How about you give me your address and I'll stop by on my way out of town tomorrow. You look for the notes you have about where they were going and then gather anything you'd like me to take to her. Sound good?"

"Oh, Libby ... I can't thank you enough!"

* * *

Alexis must have seen the look on my face as I walked Maggie Crenshaw to the front door and wished her a good day.

"Now, drink lots of water!" I called out to her as Maggie walked into the parking lot. I turned around and Alexis knew immediately that something wasn't quite right with me.

Once Maggie left the building, I turned to find my sweet little girl, Shadow, approaching me in a full-on run and with the gangly awkward legs of a growing teenager, only she is my six-month-old black Labrador Retriever.

Her hind-end was actually catching up with the front, making for a hilarious sight as I braced for impact when she jumped up to give me a hug. Even at six months, she was a stout little girl with some serious muscle and way too much energy. I scratched behind her ears and loved on her for a few moments before I looked up at Alexis.

"Do you need to sit down?" she asked me.

"That was the strangest session I've ever had. You know how we all feel more than most people?" I asked.

"How do you mean?" she said, looking at me suspiciously.

"Well, like we've talked about before … whatever mood a client is in can easily rub off on us. As therapists, or healers, it happens. We absorb feelings."

"Oh, yeah. Happens all the time with me."

"Have you experienced *visions* associated with those feelings? Do you *see* things?"

"Uh, no. Can't say that I have."

I didn't elaborate. She was going to think I was off my rocker. Instead, I walked over to the fruit-infused water dispenser we kept on the front counter and poured more water into the bottle I always carry with me. After a nice long drink of cucumber water, I started typing my session notes into the computer at the front desk.

Alexis interrupted my thoughts. "While you were in your session, the governor announced that he has signed an executive order and all non-essential businesses are being shut down for at least thirty days."

My head snapped around, astonished. "What? Why? Because of the virus?"

"Yes. We are not considered essential, unfortunately."

"We're therapists. People rely on us to keep their bodies

healthy. You know we both have clients that regularly rely on us to keep them mobile, to keep them *healthy*. What are they going to do?"

"I know, I know." Alexis was clearly distressed and it appeared to me that this was more than just about our client's health.

"What aren't you telling me?" I asked.

"You know we've been struggling since we opened to be able to turn a consistent profit. The loans we took out to build this place … this could absolutely destroy our business."

This defeatist attitude coming from Alexis was a bit shocking. She is the most positive person I've ever met. From the time we met during our massage therapy schooling, I swear she's never uttered one negative position on anything we've discussed. I always describe her as my hippie friend. She's a naturally beautiful soul, all of her five-foot nine-inch frame and the deepest brown eyes that speak with volumes of kindness behind them. Being of Asian-African American descent, although born and raised in the United States, her family ancestral lines reveal so much about her becoming a conscious healer—through meditation, massage, and the way she cares for every single living thing on the planet. She's a gracious human being who fixes *everything* and *everyone*.

"We aren't going to let our business die. We both know that we'll do whatever it takes to continue being there for our patients. Let's just get creative." After I stated the obvious, because this is how we always handle everything, her eyes seemed to relax and I got one of her huge illuminating smiles that brightens up everything around her.

"Yes, you're right, and I'm sorry that I went all

doomsday on you. We will figure things out. For now, let's wrap up our notes, clean up, and get out of here. I've got to pick up Joshua, the schools are closing down too … which also means after-school care."

Joshua was the cutest five-year-old. He was the perfect mix of his beautiful hippie mother and his tough police officer father. I introduced Jeff Johnson (we call him JJ) to Alexis almost eight years ago, and I will admit, that was the best thing I've ever done. They are a perfect little family unit.

I finished my typing at the computer and as I walked down the hallway toward the room of my last session, I couldn't help but remember the strange feelings I had around Maggie Crenshaw. I shook off the chill that suddenly gripped me and continued to strip the sheets off the table. After spraying all surfaces down with an organic disinfectant, I hefted all the linens to the laundry room and started the washing cycle.

Generally, we always try to keep an intern from the local vocational school to help us with cleaning after each client and to maintain the front desk. Monday was Sue's day off though, so Alexis and I were perfectly happy doing the grunt work.

"I suppose it's not a problem for me to hit the trails for the next two days since we have to close the doors anyway?" I mentioned to Alexis as I passed the room she was cleaning.

"Yeah, sure …you said earlier you were heading to the hills. Where are you going this time?" she asked.

"To the Rim."

"You always go there, why not try something new?"

"Oh, I will, but you know it's closest for me to escape

for a couple days and then be back for my clients. And, I forgot to tell you, but Maggie's daughter went camping up that way and hasn't called her mother. I told her I'd do what I can to reach out to her and ask her to phone home."

"That's nice of you. Doesn't she seem a little overbearing with her twenty-something?" Alexis asked.

"I hadn't really thought of that before today, but yes. I was off on my own and didn't spend a ton of time around my mom when I was her age. I wanted to be free and seek adventure. No way I was spending all my time with a parent. It does seem odd, but I guess she has a really close relationship to her, so that's really sweet."

"Ok, I'm heading out to get Josh. I plan to be back here in the morning to catch up on paperwork. … but, anything else I can do for you before I take off?"

"Nope, I'm right behind you. I need to transfer laundry loads. Maybe you could fold the load from the dryer in the morning?"

"Sure, not a problem. Have a great evening!" she shouted back through the closing door.

After locking up and getting Shadow loaded into our silver 4-Runner, I remembered that I needed to stop by Maggie's to get Isobel's medicines and whatever notes she had about where they were staying. *Now, where did I put her address?* Ah, there … corner pocket of my bag. Dharma Inspired Day Spa is located in the northeast part of Mesa and, according to my GPS, it would take twenty minutes to get to her house in central Mesa.

* * *

As soon as I pulled up, I was a little bit shocked to

see the condition of the house she lived in. It looked to be a tri-level house, as I noticed there were windows at ground level that indicated perhaps there was a basement. The grayish paint was peeling off the house and the rotting trim. There was a myriad of broken-down vehicles in the front yard, and stuff everywhere. Wow, I had no idea. It looked as though once upon a time she had a lawn, but now it was mostly dirt with some sporadic patches of crispy brown dried-up grass.

The neighborhood was a little rough looking and reminded me that I didn't know much about the Crenshaws. Funny, how one makes up opinions in their head about people without even knowing them. Maggie has been a client of mine since we opened our spa, and she sees me at least twice a month. We are not exactly a cheap day spa either so I assumed ... *wait, who is that?*

A scruffy looking man came out her front door. He was large, both in height and weight. The black long hair was sprinkled with some gray and was held back with a pony tail. His scraggly beard was mostly gray. She's not married, she told me that. *Interesting, is this a boyfriend then? Maybe a neighbor helping her out?* I got out of my vehicle and proceeded up the dirt lined walkway to the front patio.

"Can I help you?" scruffy man asked.

"I'm here to see Maggie, is she home?"

"Who are you?" he grumped.

"Libby. Libby Madsen." I extended my hand out to greet, but he abruptly turned to grab the door handle without any niceties. *Wow.*

Nearly ripping the hinges off the screened door, he entered the house. After the slam of the door hitting the frame, I heard a bellowing "MAGGIE! There's a Libby here to see you!"

I waited on the decrepit wooden front porch. I heard footsteps approaching and prayed they weren't his.

"Libby! I nearly forgot you were stopping by this evening. Come in, come in," Maggie said in a gracious manner.

Walking into their house, I noticed that the grump had flopped down in his recliner and was nursing a beer as he watched some news on TV. She made no attempt to introduce me or explain who he was. I swear he turned the volume up higher as we began to talk.

"You said you had notes about where your daughter was headed to? And something about medication?" I reminded Maggie.

"John, TURN DOWN THE VOLUME!" Maggie screamed at him. I jumped, completely startled with eyes wide open. I didn't know she had a voice like that. *What the hell?*

He did turn down the volume slightly. Then, with the sweetest voice, and as though she hadn't just turned into Satan momentarily, she turned to me. "Yes, right here." She walked to the kitchen counter and amazingly found a little notepad among the very cluttered surface. "And, here in the fridge is an extra bottle of insulin." She handed both to me and started to usher me toward the front door. It was clear that even though she didn't apologize for her living conditions, she wasn't exactly comfortable with me there either.

"Ok, I plan on leaving early tomorrow morning. I'll call you once I've made contact with her. Have a great evening," I said, eager to get home now.

The whole way home, I couldn't shake how odd it was

to see Maggie when everything she had told me to date painted a completely different picture in my mind. And, who was that man? How could they live with all that stuff everywhere, inside and out? I drove home feeling extremely grateful for my life and also really wanting to help Maggie. My instincts were kicking in and I sensed that not everything was as it seemed. Was there something more going on with her daughter than an innocent camping trip with her friends? Are Maggie and Isobel safe with behemoth man?

CHAPTER THREE

The drive up north to the Rim was uneventful. I looked in the rearview mirror to the backseat where Shadow was curled up and fast asleep on the seat. My thoughts wandered as I wound my way through the mountain terrain, observing the vast pine tree wilderness as I crested the final climb onto what Arizonans know famously as the Mogollon Rim. Known for its majestic forests of ponderosa pine, and a similar flora and fauna to the Rocky Mountain range, the elevation here can be 4,000 feet on the southern slopes and all the way to 8,000 feet to the north. Zane Grey, the western novelist, even had a hunting cabin on the Rim back in history.

I was familiar with this area, as I have been exploring it all from a very young age. My father and I used to come here camping, fishing, and hiking since I was old enough to walk. We loved spending time in nature and were always hesitant to head back into the city. My father was an insurance broker and worked himself to death. Literally. His sudden heart attack when I was nearing my sixteenth birthday completely devastated me.

Shaking my head to keep that memory from coming back, I passed a sign indicating that the turnoff was in one mile. Soon, I saw it—the sign saying *Young—19 miles*. I started to slow down to make the turn onto Hwy 188. Tuesdays were great days for camping; there were few people around. I love the solitude. On the right-hand side of the road, less than a mile, I saw the turnoff I was looking for. *Perfect, I just want to find Isobel, have her call her mother, and then I'll get on with my hike for the rest of the day.*

I noticed there were a few more campers down this road, but all in all, it was mostly quiet. On both sides, there were thick pine trees and beautiful large oak. The squirrels were busy as ever, scurrying about gathering their nuts and climbing up the trees.

I turned onto the forest road and saw a sign with 'Camp Host' about 100 feet on the right. *Camp Host? Since when did they put camp hosts in this area—that's new.* Well, might as well stop and ask them … that'd be the quickest way to find Isobel. As I pulled up in front of a thirty-foot silver trailer, I saw that they also had an old white beat-up Ford pickup and a red side-by-side vehicle for getting around the campground. It had a rake, shovel, and a bucket attached to the roll bar behind the passenger seat.

I started getting out. "Shadow, no, you need to stay here for a few more minutes. Then we'll go find our own camp site and I'll let you out. Be right back." That was the important instruction for her, *'be right back'*, said with my index finger straight up in front of her face and with the 'serious voice' meant she was sure to get a cookie when I returned. *If* she behaved and followed the command.

"Hello!" I yelled out when I didn't see any obvious sign of people out and about.

The door to the silver trailer flew open and a lady with long, stringy, blonde hair stepped out shielding her eyes from the sun that hit her face. "Hi, be right there. Let me get my shoes on," she yelled back.

As I waited, I saw evidence that they, too, had a dog. Of course they did, this is a wonderful place for canines to spend their summers. I didn't actually see what kind of dog, just the evidence of a lead tied to a tree, water and food bowls outside the door.

"Sorry about that, I'm usually out the door much earlier than this, but my husband agreed to head out first this morning to give me a little break."

"I'm surprised to see camp hosts here at all. I've been coming up here most of my life and have never seen these dispersed areas to have hosts."

"Yeah, the forest service is in dire need of hosts now. Seems everyone is finding camping as the cheaper entertainment these days. And, I imagine, with the pandemic it will only get worse. No better way to socially distance than be out here among nature." Her accent I couldn't place exactly, but my bets were somewhere from the south, maybe even Kentucky?

"I'm actually looking for some friends and I'm hoping maybe you've seen them and could point me toward their camp? A blonde girl in her twenties with a couple others of similar age?" It was then I realized I didn't have great descriptions, or names; in fact, I really didn't have much at all. That was really dumb that I didn't ask. I'd seen Isobel before when she came into the spa, but I wouldn't say I was recollecting great detail.

"Well, these days, there's lots of them younguns camping. Could be any one of 'em, really." She pointed out. "There are maybe about four camp sites being used right now at our campground, most people pulled out Sunday. Just drive on down and see if you find who you're looking for."

That didn't go as easily as I thought it would. In my mind, I guess I expected to be told exactly where to look, I'd drive there and find her, give her the extra meds and dial up her mom so they could talk. Shadow was getting antsy, so I decided we'd find our own camp site first and get set up, then walk along the road so we got exercise while looking for Isobel and her friends.

* * *

I was fortunate to have a pup that stayed right by me everywhere I went. From the moment I got her, she has stayed by my side. If we're around people we don't know, or on hiking trails, I'll leash her. In our own camp site, I rarely have to. Shadow was racing around smelling everything as I set up our tent. She was in heaven.

Once we set out for our walk, I put her leash on just in case there were other dogs around. Never want to invite trouble. It was a gorgeous day with the sun shining, but the temperatures were so much cooler than down in the valley. We could actually be here walking in the sun without our skin getting torched.

The first campsite had an RV parked and looked like a couple in their sixties maybe. Definitely not the kids I was

looking for. There was another site across the road from
them, on my left, that looked promising. It had a blue tent,
a camp table with a Coleman stove on top, and a couple
chairs sitting out. No people were visible. They could be
in the tent, I suppose. Then again, there was no car so
probably not. It was more of a hike down the road to
the next ones. Everything here was spaced out where you
couldn't see one site from another—exactly what I loved
about this place.

Shadow's nose was in overdrive, sniffing all the
wonderful nature smells along the way. Suddenly, she
stopped, pointed her nose toward the forest and let out
a piercing bark. She looked at me and then tugged to go
that way.

"What is it, girl?"

Shadow growled and pulled at the leash. We walked
closer to the edge of the trees and just as my girl growled
again, something ran. It was dark in the trees so I couldn't
see exactly what it was. An animal? A person? The noise it
made seemed larger than what a squirrel or skunk would
make, but I couldn't be sure.

"C'mon, girl ... let's go back to the road."

As we walked, I heard more rustling of the forest floor
leaves and then some kind of vehicle started. A quad?
The camp host cart? We kept walking; obviously it was
just campers. *So why am I so jumpy all of a sudden.* As the
road rounded into a sharper turn, a side-by-side appeared
quickly out of nowhere and nearly collided with us.

"Hey! Watch it!" I yelled out.

The man stopped and got out of his buggy. Every hair
on Shadow's back and neck bristled—standing straight up.
My radar was definitely telling me something.

"I wanted to make sure you slow down, there can be kids and dogs along this road. We don't want anyone to get hurt." I said in a calmer voice now.

He stared at me for an awkwardly long few seconds, and as I was getting quite uncomfortable, he broke out in a big smile.

"Hi! I'm Charlie. My woman and me are hosts at this here campground. I'm glad you are watching out for all of us too. You're right, I was going way too fast ... excited to get my work done and head off to the lake for some fishin'."

If I'd thought his wife had stringy long blonde hair, this guy was her identical twin. Pasty white skin, brilliant blue eyes, small frame, skinny. When he smiled, I could see there were few teeth that remained in place. The two or three that showed were discolored. I'm sure his breath reeked. I took a step or so back to maintain distance.

"Hi Charlie. I'm Libby, and this is my dog Shadow. I think we talked to your wife a little bit ago. I explained to her we're looking for a group of twenty-somethings that are supposed to be camping along here. You wouldn't have seen them up the road there where you just came from, would you?" My senses were settling down. Shadow's were not.

"Nope. Nobody down thataway," he quickly replied.

"Ok, we'll continue walking for exercise then. Thank you!" I started to turn to head off when I noticed the mud on his shoes and I realized how much his hands were shaking. Odd. *Maybe he's flustered by my beauty. Ha! Libby, you're such the comedian, aren't you?*

"Nothing more to see down thataway. Might as well head back for camp."

He's oddly insistent, isn't he?

"Thank you."

He started up his side-by-side and sped off. I watched after him until I lost sight and all the dust had dissipated. *He sure is a weird little man.* No matter, we're going to continue our walk anyway.

Charlie was right, there was nothing more to see down the way. I realized that the first two sites before the camp hosts and then the two after where Shadow and I set up camp were the only occupied sites in the place. After over an hour of walking and enjoying nature, Shadow's tongue seemed to be hanging lower out of her mouth ... always an indication it's time for a break and some water.

We walked back toward the site with the blue tent and as we approached, I yelled out "Hello, campers!" It's always a good idea to announce your approach. Most people camping in Arizona are packing heat and you never want to surprise them.

It was quiet and there was no sign of life. I truly wanted to snoop a bit around their camp, but again, there is etiquette to observe, so that would not be the brightest thing to do. We headed on back to our own site instead.

Shadow was pooped. After drinking a bowl of water and eating her kibble, she sacked out on the doggie bed I set up just outside the tent. I was sitting in my chair reading *The Henna Artist* when I looked up to find the camp hosts.

"Hello!" the thin identical twins yelled out in unison as they approached.

"Oh, hello!" I waved and got up to meet them closer to the road. "Shadow, wait!" I commanded with my palm straight up in front of her. Shadow sat and watched. "Good girl!"

"Did you find your friends?" the lady asked.

"No, unfortunately, I didn't. By the way, my name is Libby ... my dog over there is Shadow." I'd introduced myself to him, but never caught her name earlier.

"Hi, I'm Julie and you've met Charlie from what I understand." *Was that a hint of irritation I detected in her voice?*

"Nice to meet you. I really like what you're doing around here. I could tell instantly the camp sites are cleaned up and there isn't as much garbage lying about. I swear, every time I come up here, I end up carrying out at least one large bag of other people's trash. Thank you for all you're doing to keep our forests clean." I really did notice a huge difference.

Her demeanor instantly changed and she appeared to be much more approachable. "Oh, of course, that's what we're here for. It is amazing, isn't it, that people can't clean up after themselves. We've started taking down license plate numbers and reporting offenders to the officials. Not that they have time to do anything about it, but at least it's something more than before." Julie said in that certain drawl I noticed earlier.

"Hey, do you know who has the blue tent two campsites down from here?" I remembered I still hadn't seen anyone drive by, so I believed it was still unoccupied.

"Haven't seen them in several days. Some hikers, so I imagine they're on a day hike and will be back," Charlie answered.

"Do you remember what they look like? About how old?" I asked.

"Ummm, not really." Julie and Charlie answered, again almost in unison. *How weird is that?*

"Alright, I'll have to take a drive around the surrounding camps and see if I can locate my friends."

"The reason we stopped by … we generally invite the campers over to our space every Tuesday evening for a s'mores fest just after supper time. There ain't many around this week, but you're more than welcome to join us, if you'd like." Julie offered.

"That's so nice of you and I'll keep that in mind." I didn't want to obligate myself to anything. I haven't had the most positive vibes from these two so I definitely wanted to leave a way out.

"Sounds good. The local forest ranger usually joins us too. Real nice guy," Charlie added as they headed back toward their trailer.

Well, that would be interesting. I'd love to talk to a ranger and determine if maybe he'd seen our lost campers. Maybe I would join them after all.

Shadow did a wonderful job of staying put while they were in our camp. I was amazed since she was still such a young exuberant pup. I gave her extra treats and showered her with love and she ate it all up.

* * *

In the early afternoon, we took a drive. First, in case I missed those hikers driving by, we drove by their camp again. Still no sign of life. On the way over to a little town called Heber, I called Maggie using the hands-free feature.

"Maggie, it's Libby. No, haven't seen them yet, but there is a campsite right near mine that I'm pretty sure could be theirs. It's been unoccupied since I arrived, but could be they're hiking. Do you know what color or brand their tent is?"

"No idea," she abruptly said.

"What kind of car were they in?"

"It's red. A sedan, I think."

"Any idea on make or model?"

"Nope."

Was it me, or was Maggie just not helpful in a situation where I was doing her a favor? I was starting to get irritated, but decided it wasn't worth it. After a few more short and curt answers, I said goodbye and promised to call if I learned anything more.

* * *

Shadow and I continued driving through campgrounds and then headed down Hwy 260 toward Heber. It was particularly gorgeous today, as cumulus clouds were building in the distance forming against the deep blue skies, as only found in the Southwest. Shadow seemed to have similar thoughts as she gazed out the window, with the wind and a smile on her face. Good times. There were deer grazing in the field off to my right and cows and horses on a ranch to my left and that was the scene for several miles.

The speed limit slowed way down as I approached the edge of town. I saw a Circle K. Perfect, I needed to grab a few things … namely, s'mores ingredients: graham crackers, marshmallows, and chocolate bars, so I pulled in. I also figured it'd be nice if I showed up with a little something for the hosts … a six-pack of beer should do it. Nothing fancy. They definitely were not the wine sort of fancy.

As I approached the counter with my goods, I noticed a red sedan filling up with gas at the pumping bay outside the window. The young man looked to be in his twenties, brown hair, a bit disheveled. I really wished Maggie could have been more descriptive about these friends. Who am I looking for? How many? Were there both male and female friends along for this journey? Anyway, this red sedan only had the one young male, no Isobel. I did take note of the license plate though as I walked back to my car. Pretending to take a selfie, I snapped a picture and hopefully it captured the whole plate behind me. Why anyone would snap a selfie at Circle K, I don't know, but no one seemed to even notice me.

It was a short drive back to the campground and the second we stopped and I opened the door, Shadow leaped down and ran around as though she'd been locked up all day. Her sniffer was on the move; no stone was left unturned when finally, she was done patrolling our temporary homestead.

Did I leave the tent unzipped? Surely, I checked that before I left, I thought as I walked over to it. Looking inside, nothing appeared to be missing or disheveled ... everything was in its place. *That's strange, how careless of me.*

* * *

The evening was gorgeous. Temperature was not too hot or too cold. In the western sky, the clouds cast a pinkish-orange hue that kept turning different shades of yellows, reds, and gold. You'd swear the horizon was on fire, but then it'd turn deep pink before fading away.

"It's really difficult to look away from, isn't it?" a deep voice over my right shoulder startled me.

I jumped. "OH! Wow, you startled me! I didn't even hear anyone walk up." Goosebumps popped up on my arms and my heart raced wildly. I suppose I really was lost in the sunset. Now I was looking at the most gorgeous man I'd ever laid eyes on. Both took my breath away.

"I apologize, I truly thought you heard me approach. I didn't mean to startle ... uh, I'm Greg Lawson with the USDA-Forest Service." He looked flustered.

After a deep breath and regulating my heart that had jumped into my throat two seconds ago, I smiled and reached my hand out in greeting, "I'm Libby Madsen. Camping a couple spaces up the road from here." I couldn't remove my gaze from his astonishingly gorgeous eyes. It was like staring into the crystal-clear Caribbean sea. *Stop it, Libby ... look away!*

"Nice to meet you, ma'am, and again I'm sorry I scared you so bad."

"Oh, er, uh ... no worries. Guess I'm a bit jumpy. That sunset is stunning, isn't it? We don't get them this nice down in the valley."

"Is that where you're from? Phoenix?" he inquired.

"Mesa actually, yes." *Why am I so flustered? Get yourself together, Libby.*

"Well, I'm headed over to the fire with the others to get in on that s'mores action. You comin'?" He turned and started walking toward Julie and Charlie, who were standing by the campfire, talking to the couple in their sixties that I'd seen earlier.

"Do you come every Tuesday for s'mores night?" I inquired, as I skipped a bit to catch up with him.

"Not every week, but I try to connect with all the folks around here as often as I can. It helps build rapport in the community, and we find people less likely to trash our forests when we engage directly with them. That's why we also started placing camp hosts this year."

"Yes, I was telling Julie earlier how much I appreciate that they're here. They've made a big difference." I still couldn't take my eyes out of that ocean. They were impossible to look away from.

"Indeed, they are doing a great job here. So that means you have been up here before?" He slowed to a stop and turned to me with his question.

"Since I was a child. Fished over at Willow and Woods Canyon a lot with my dad when I was younger. Hiked all over the entire area. I feel most at home right here in the forest, not down in the city."

"Then why don't you move up here?" he asked.

"My business is in Mesa and it is like my baby, can't ever see leaving it. But, I do spend my time off up here, or traveling wherever my Trina takes me."

"Is Trina your daughter?"

"Oh, no … Trina is my trusted Toyota 4-Runner that takes me anywhere I feel led to go." I blushed, realizing how I shared one of my biggest quirks with this man.

Laughing out loud, "You name your vehicle?" he asked.

"Of course. You don't?"

"No, haven't ever done that. I will say though, you have good taste in cars."

I followed his eyes as he gazed over at his truck … a white Toyota Tundra.

"Well, look at that! They are reliable, aren't they? Love mine."

Just then, a roar of laughter over at the fire pit infiltrated our conversation and we both remembered where we were headed.

"Let's go see what all the laughter is about over there, shall we?" he suggested.

I wasn't sure if the tingling feeling in my belly had to do with the beer I was drinking or the easy conversation. Regardless, I was having a great time. It was good to get away from the locked-down city and still share stories with people in an outdoor setting and not worry about the darn pandemic that seemed to be taking so many lives so quickly.

As I looked around the campfire, I realized in this moment that connection was exactly what I've been needing as of late. Here are some seemingly nice people; none of which I knew twenty-four hours ago, but now we laughed as though we'd known each other forever. It was right about that time, I noticed a young man in the group that I hadn't been introduced to. I started heading that direction when all of a sudden, he bolted, right into the darkness of the forest. *What? What just happened? Did anyone else notice?* No, I looked around and no one seemed to notice.

Walking up to Julie, I asked, "Who was the young man standing over there a second ago? He seemed to leave quickly."

She looked all around and with a puzzled look on her face, she turned to me and asked, "Which young man? I don't remember there being anyone else here?"

"He was right there. Had a red hoodie on?"

"How much beer have you had, Libby?" she laughed and walked away.

I was still nursing the *one* beer I arrived with. I know it's not that. *Maybe Greg saw what I did?*

I casually walked over to where he and Charlie were talking.

"Well, howdy Libby … you enjoyin' yerself?" Charlie slurred.

"Oh, yes, this has been a very enjoyable evening. Thank

you for doing this. Hey, do you know who that young man with the red hoodie was? He was over there, but ran off suddenly?" I was pointing into the dark tree line.

The puzzled look on both of their faces told me they had no clue what I was talking about. *Ok, don't make any more fuss over this. These people are going to think you are a bit crazy.*

"Ok. Well, I'm going to call it a night. It's been a long day and Shadow and I plan on a nice long hike tomorrow. Thanks again for the invite and I'll see you tomorrow." I turned, pulled my flashlight out of my pocket, and headed off down the road toward my tent.

Gorgeous blue eyes quickly caught up to me. "Hey, tomorrow is my day off and I was wondering if I might join you on that hike?"

Yes, yes, yes! Of course!

"Well, honestly, before my dog and I set off for hiking, we've got to find this daughter of a friend of mine. She needs to call her worried mom and I have some medication for her since she's overdue from her camping trip."

"There's a missing person? Did you call it in?" he quickly asked.

"Um, I'm not sure she's actually missing. Her mom is worried, but she's a grown adult and camping with her friends. The battery on her phone probably died and her mother's overbearing tendencies have kicked in. Since I'm up here anyway, I told her mom I'd check in on her."

"Hmmm. Ok. I do have resources and I could help you out. Here's my card in case you'd like to reach me. I mean it, I'd be happy to help." Looking a bit dejected, he slowly walked away and disappeared into the darkness out of reach of my flashlight's beam.

Why didn't you invite him along for the search, Libby? For reasons I just don't really understand yet myself, I always back away from potentially great men. It's my way.

* * *

Wednesday morning, I awoke refreshed after great sleep in the crisp, cool air. Shadow and I apparently snuggled through the night and I don't think either one of us budged a bit. I slowly started to move and my sweet girl rolled on her back, indicating I'm to rub her belly for a bit before I'm allowed to crawl over her and out of the tent. I spent some time doing just that, stroking her belly and giving her a gentle massage ... waking up each of her parts: her tummy, each of her legs, those adorable floppy ears, and then I massaged around her forehead, nose, and chin. She stretched really long and then bounced up and we both headed out of the tent. Shadow ran to the edge of our camp and did her business while I searched my car for the camp stove, the kettle, and the coffee grounds. Where did I put that French press? Ah, there it is ... all ready for the perfect cup of coffee.

Shadow came back raring to go, so much spunk in this girl, I don't fully know where she gets all her energy. I poured the boiling water over the coffee grounds in my French press and waited the obligatory five minutes for it to steep.

"Bring me your ball, girl." I knew once I started this, it could go on for hours. "Good girl, that's a really good girl," I said in my sweet high-pitched voice that gets her so excited.

As I played with her and drank my coffee, I started

going over everything I'd done over the past twenty-four hours. Maggie told me she was worried about her daughter. I had that weird sensation and vision. The scruffy man at her house was a surprise and somehow, I didn't trust him at all.

Then, in the mountains, I met the camp hosts and the super gorgeous forest ranger. I'm still on the fence with the camp hosts. Julie and Charlie were friendly and they sure have done a lot to help this campground, but there was a nagging bit in the back of my head. He seems shady. *Oh, c'mon Libby! Just because you don't understand some types doesn't make them bad people.*

Wait a minute, what is that over there? A campfire? If I'm not mistaken, that is probably where the empty tent was. "Shadow, come here ... come on, girl! Let's go for walk!" She bolted my direction and I clipped on her leash.

Walking along the road, and as we turned on a slight bend, I could now see the camp. There was someone there now! Or, at least there was a red car, the blue tent flap was open a little, and there was a fire in their fire pit. I kept looking in anticipation of seeing people, but so far, no one. We started walking slower, then I bent down pretending to tie my shoe while I was getting a better look at the car. *Was that the one I saw at Circle K yesterday?* It had really faded red paint, a few bumper stickers on the back, and what I could see of the license plate, it started with what looked to be LT, but then the rest was difficult to see because the whole back end was covered in mud. *I wonder what that picture I took shows?*

Shadow started barking and a young man with a hoodie on came walking toward us, but not from the campground, he was on the road.

"Hi there!" I said.

"Mornin'," he muttered.

"Hey, listen … you don't know an Isobel by chance, do you?

He stared at me like I was an idiot, but didn't say anything at all. He walked right on by me. *What the … ? Rude!*

"Excuse me, I was wondering if you may have seen…" he kept walking and was not listening to me at all. Then it hit me, he was wearing a red hoodie. *Was he the same one from around the fire last night?*

"Hey! Why are you ignoring me? I just want to ask a couple simple questions." Nope, he went straight for his car, got in it, and sped off toward the main highway kicking up a ton of dust in the process. I was stunned.

His campfire was still burning strong, too, so I hurried over to our camp hosts to inform them. I certainly didn't have enough water with me to put out their fire. Shadow and I were jogging by this point. I heard that Charlie must have started up one of his buggy's and was headed our direction.

"Well, yur sure up early for a mornin' jog," he said, slowing down when he got to us.

Breathlessly, I muttered, "Yes, did you see that red car that sped by?"

"I did. So I thought I'd see if I need to clean the camp site."

"Well, that's the same hoodie guy I saw last night at your place. Remember, the one I was asking if you knew? He ran into the woods when I tried to approach him?" The expression on his face told me everything, he barely remembered last night. "Ok, well, I was simply trying to ask him this morning if he had seen my friends … he quickly got in his car and roared away. Something is not right."

"Did he pack up his gear?" he asked.

"No! That's just it. His tent and camping gear are all still there. He left a roaring fire! Which is why we're running over to your place. Do you have water and can you bring a shovel to put that fire out?"

"Of course, no problem. Let me grab water back at the trailer and I'll get 'er done."

"Do you mind if we go with you? Can we hop on and get a ride?"

"Sure, no problem at all. Get on in, Libby. Let's go put us a fahr out." Shadow and I jumped on and Charlie took off. We grabbed a few five-gallon pails of water and loaded them on the small 'truck bed' like space on his side-by-side. Off we went to the abandoned fire.

Oh boy, that fire was huge now. What an idiot, leaving it burning. What on earth was that guy's problem? Charlie stopped and jumped off, grabbing his shovel and water. I grabbed two pails and followed him. We poured water, stirred it up with the shovel, poured more and stirred again. It was still really hot when you hovered your hands above the charcoal soup we'd made.

"I've gotta go get more water; can you just keep stirring? Maybe shovel somma that sand right over there yonder on it?" Charlie asked me.

"Sure, no problem."

As he went to leave and I shoveled a couple scoops of sand into the hot, fiery pit, I noticed that Shadow was making herself at home in this camp. She was headlong into the tent when I looked up.

"Hey, Shadow … what are you doing? Get out of

there!" I put the shovel down and went over to my dog. She was all the way in now. *Well, I'm not purposely breaking and entering. I'm simply retrieving my nosey dog. Right?*

I bent down to look in. She was rubbing and nosing all through the sleeping bag and some of the clothes that were strewn around. "Shadow! Get over here! Get out!" I called to her, but she was rolling around and acting as though this was hers to play in. I crawled in, attempting to grab the harness she had on (we call it a bra). After missing a couple times, and falling right into the center of the tent and a pile of clothes, I rolled over feeling something hard hit under my right hip. As I felt around, I pulled out a knife. I really large, hunting knife.

I heard a vehicle approaching and my heart stopped. *Please don't let it be red hoodie guy!* I peeked out and saw Charlie's old beater Ford pulling in.

"What're doin' in someone else's tent, Libby?" Charlie yelled out, almost scolding me.

"Shadow went snooping in there and I was just trying to get her out." I replied, almost embarrassed, and as though I was a school kid getting caught by the principal. "Hey, is it hunting season?"

"No, why?"

"Just wondered."

He'd brought back several more pails full of water and we got that fire completely drowned. Shadow was now consumed with treeing a squirrel. One ran up a tree not far from us, and she was not going to let it come back down.

"Had you met this camper yet?" I asked Charlie.

"Can't say I have."

"So, you still don't remember that he was at the s'mores gathering last night?"

"Nope, couldn't really say I saw him."

Is this guy freakin' blind? I wanted to scream, but didn't.

"Well, our work is done here. I'll watch fer him to come back and then give 'em a warnin' for leaving that fire. I'll also report it to Greg this mornin'" Charlie informed me.

We all jumped in his truck and he dropped us off at our camp. By the time we got there, I had decided to pull out Greg's card and give him a call. I wanted to make sure this did get reported, plus I wanted to show him the picture from the gas station to see if that helped.

For some reason, I wasn't comfortable sharing that with Charlie. Maybe Mr. Forest Ranger would still be open for going on a hike with us today, too? *Nope, the butterflies were not because of the beer last night,* I thought, as they fluttered through my stomach just thinking of the hunky ranger.

CHAPTER FOUR

As I watched the Tundra pull in, my heart skipped a beat. *What are you doing, Libby? How many times does this type of thing go horribly wrong before you get it that you aren't good in relationships?*

His door shutting snapped me back to reality.

"Good morning!" he yelled from the truck.

"Hiya! Oh, Shadow, stop jumping. Get back here. C'mon."

"She's ok, I love dogs. She's a sweetie," he assured me.

"Let me grab a light jacket and my day pack. Wanna take mine or yours?"

"Oh, we'll take Whitey, no problem," he informed with a bit of a grin on his face.

"Oh! You named him now, did ya?" I teased. "As long as you don't mind a lot of black hair in your vehicle. She sheds like crazy."

"No worries at all."

"I do want to travel through some of the other campgrounds in this area to see if I run into Isobel. Do you mind that we check those out along the way?"

"Sure, not a problem."

We planned to take the road toward Young and then venture off to another campground to the east, following a ridge that overlooks a fish hatchery. It's a beautiful walk and it was a perfect day for it. Cloudless sky, temperatures were only going to be in the seventies, which is much better than at home so I was quite happy.

On our way, we slowly drove several different roads where people frequently boondock. Again, I was not entirely sure what vehicle to look for, but I was looking for any sign of a younger blonde girl. Mostly, what we saw were retirees, probably sixty-five and older. Makes sense during the middle of the week, I suppose.

"Well, we tried. Let's go take our hike and then I'll give Maggie a call and let her know I've struck out."

As we made our way to the trailhead, I was telling Greg all about the morning's adventure putting the fire out.

"Nothing makes me angrier than campers that leave their fires going when they drive away. And, he didn't take his stuff with him?" he lamented.

"No, all I did was ask him if he knew an Isobel, and then whether he may have seen my friend's daughter who I'm looking for. He never answered me. In fact, he just walked off and never said a word. Then he got in his car and sped off! I was left there speechless and stunned."

"Wow, that sounds awfully suspicious. Or, if nothing else, it was darn rude. Most people I come across are always friendly around here. I wonder what his problem is?" Greg looked concerned. "Is this the guy that you were asking us about last night near the campfire? The one who you said ran off?"

"Yes! Yes, I do think he's the one. It was pretty dark, but I swear he had a red hoodie on and so did the guy this morning." I was happy to hear I hadn't been ignored on this subject last night. *He remembered!*

Climbing up a steep incline, with Shadow far in the lead, both of us saved our oxygen and stopped talking for a bit. Once we made it to the top of the ridge, we caught our breath and marveled at the gorgeous scenery directly in front of us.

"You can see forever right here," he pointed out.

"I'll never tire of the views from the Rim, that's for sure."

I noticed Shadow pawing at something on the ground. I moved closer to see what she was doing. Her nose was buried deep into fallen leaves, and then she started digging. Something metallic flashed. *What is that?* I moved closer, bent down, and moved some oak leaves on the ground. A cell phone. At the moment that I touched the phone, I saw a clear vision of the same girl and a leaf as I had seen during Maggie's massage the other day. *What on earth?*

"Whatcha got there?" Greg asked Shadow.

"Hmm, looks like someone lost their phone up here." I wasn't going to mention the vision I just had. I'm not sure he'd understand. I turned to the dog, "Good girl, Shadow! Look what you found. Someone will be happy you found this." I gave her a treat from my pocket and rubbed her ears.

"We have a lost and found box at the ranger station, I

can take it with me."

"It looks like a similar Samsung as mine, I'd like to charge it and see if I can get in and discover who it belongs to first. But, yes, if we can't figure it out, then by all means we'll put it in the lost and found box."

After several more minutes of staring at the vast wilderness in front of us, eating an apple, and drinking more water, we decided to begin our descent. As we made our way down the trail, we both noticed a ranch house far off in the distance.

"I didn't realize anyone lived out this direction, did you?" I asked, pointing toward the ranch.

"There are a few ranches throughout this area, but nope, can't say I knew about that one specifically."

Shadow bounded ahead, not even concerned at all about her footing. Wouldn't it be nice to have four legs for balance while hiking? We'd definitely be able to move faster if we had that ability. Instead, I kept my eyes just in front of each foot, stepping carefully and testing the stability of the rock before applying my full weight and keeping my hiking poles at my side for more balance. Greg was doing the exact same thing and we made fairly good time all the way to the bottom.

Back at the car, I searched my pack for my phone charger and it did fit the phone we found. Greg had a handy USB connection in Whitey so hopefully we'd get some charge before we got back to the campground.

"When do you have to head back to the city?" Greg asked.

"Unfortunately, tonight is my last night and I'll get up real early and head home."

"Ah, that's too bad. There are many other great hikes

I could take you on if you were staying a few more days."

"I'd love that." Feeling my heart leap at the thought, I felt my face starting to flush. *Look out the window, don't let him detect your feelings, Libby.*

"I never did ask what you do for a living. It seems we've only talked about the goings on here in the hills. What takes you back to the city? Have a husband and kids left back there?" he asked, sounding like he hoped there wasn't.

"Ha! No! No, husband or kids. Just a business that my partner Alexis and I have built from the ground up. Dharma Inspired Day Spa. We're both licensed massage therapists. She has the business degree and worked in corporate for many years as an accountant, so she is our business manager and LMT."

"Partner?" he asked with a little wiggle of his eyebrows.

"Oh, no! Not as in my life partner, just business partner and best friend."

"Good," he quickly added, patting my knee and sending electricity through every nerve in my body.

Trying to recover and ignore the overtones, I continued, "She's married and has a five-year-old son—cute as can be! We both are natural healers and absolutely love what we do. The problem now is that with the pandemic, we had to close our doors this week."

"Why hurry back to the city then?"

"We need to get together and figure out how we're going to navigate this shut down. I'm praying it doesn't last more than the thirty days."

"It sure is affecting all types of business, isn't it?" he asked.

"More than you know."

We approached the campground turnoff, and that

hoodie guy's red car had turned in from the other direction. Greg noticed at the same time I did.

"I'm going to drop you off at your site, and go talk to that punk," he said with a scowl that told me it was not going to be a nice conversation.

Charlie's side by side pulled out onto the 171 road after the red car and before Whitey. *Oh, red car dude, you are so gonna get it...*

Greg quickly dropped us off, promising to be back shortly for a proper goodbye. *Fluttering heart—Stop it!*

"Shadow! No! You are not going to run after them. Get over here!" I yelled out. She was a good girl, detecting the seriousness in my voice.

The phone we found had charged to twenty-five percent during the drive. I opened up Trina and started her so I could continue charging and begin to snoop for the owner. It fired up and much to my amazement, there was no password or fingerprint needed to access. I immediately went to the phone icon on the front screen and started examining the contact list. The listing wasn't all that long actually, maybe it didn't belong to a teenager then?

Anne T.
Davis Heating & Plumbing
Grandma
Heather
Mom
Tom
Work

First, I tried 'Mom' since that seemed most obvious way to quickly discover the owner of this device. No answer, and oddly enough, no voice message either. *Dangit.* Then, I started at the top of the list, no answer for Anne. Davis

Heating had no idea whose phone number this was and had no patience for me (*remind me never to use that company!*). Grandma, no answer, but I did leave a message. Heather was at work, or at least that's what the man who hung up on me informed. No answer with Tom, but I did achieve a bit of success with the number labeled 'work'.

"Good morning! You've reached Quality Computers, how may I help you?" a perky young woman's voice sounded so cheerful when she answered.

"Yes, I found a cellphone with 'work' listed in the contacts. I'm hoping you can help me find the owner?" I explained.

"Uh, oh ... I really thought this might be Bella calling, given the number that popped up on my display. This isn't Bella?" the young girl asked.

"No, my name is Libby, and I'm a hiker who found this phone in the mountains this morning while hiking. Are you telling me it belongs to a Bella?" *Bella ... Isobel. Crap! It is her phone! Or maybe that's a good thing? Then we know she really is up here?*

"Oh. Hi, my name is Heather. Yes, this is her number. Oh boy. She lost her phone? She went off camping with her boyfriend a few days ago. We were getting kind of worried because she was due back at work yesterday. She has never missed a day of work since she started here two years ago. She lo..."

Boyfriend?

"Heather," I had to interrupt, "do you know her boyfriend well? What's his name? Could you describe him to me, or the vehicle they were traveling in?"

Long sigh. "Oh wait, hold on, the other line is ringing and I have to get it."

As I was waiting for Heather to come back on the line, I saw dust billowing on the road. The red car was flying at a high rate of speed. It wasn't long before I saw Greg's truck, and then in that cloud of dust, Charlie's little putt-putt was chugging along too, with him squinting, trying to see where he was going. *What in the world is going on here? Guess they are literally chasing him out of town. Poor Charlie, how can he even breathe?*

"Sorry, Libby, it's been a busy day here at work. Uh, Rod … what can I say about Rod? I can't say I care too much for him, he's a player. I told her she's too good for him. I mean, who goes camping with someone they've never met in person?"

Playing along and not showing any surprise about this new development about a boyfriend, I kept my voice calm, cool, and collected. "They never met in person? Did she ever share a picture of him? Can you please describe what he *looks* like? What car does he drive?"

"Oh, yeah … she showed me a picture once. He has unkempt brown hair. Skinny dude. I don't know that I've seen his car … maybe Bella told me it was orange, or red, or… oh, I can't remember."

"Her mother thought she had gone camping with a group of friends from work. Did you know about that?"

"No. Bella told me that she was meeting up with Rod. No one else from here are really friends with her and I can't imagine any of them *camping*." Heather made camping sound like a dirty word.

"Thank you, Heather. You've been a big help." I said, hanging up, with a sick feeling in my stomach. *Oh boy, I think I've been camping near this Rod the whole time. And, I think he just sped away… but, where is Isobel?*

CHAPTER FIVE

"Isobel!!??" Maggie cried out.

"Uh, no. I'm sorry, Maggie. This is Libby."

"This is Isobel's phone number! I saw I had a missed call from her. Why are you answering her phone? Let me talk to her. Now!"

"Maggie. Please. Take a deep breath."

"Don't tell me what to do. Just put my daughter on the phone!" She was clearly distraught and not wanting to face reality.

"Maggie, I'm sorry. I found Isobel's phone while hiking earlier this morning. We haven't found her yet, but there is a search team being assembled at this moment." I tried to explain plainly and succinctly since I knew she was frantic.

"Who's 'we'?" she responded.

"Forest service rangers, search and rescue, and the

state police."

"Why? Why … do they think something bad has happened to her?"

"We did find one of her friends. He's being detained by the state police at the moment, but he's not talking."

There was a long pause. "*HE!?* There were *boys* with her?" she asked, each word was dripping with disgust.

"That's what we are trying to figure out. Listen, you stay tight right where you are. I will call you as soon as we learn anything more, ok?"

"I want to come up there!"

"Please, Maggie … she may still come home so we need you there in case she does," I pleaded.

"Ok, please call me. Keep me informed. Oh, I can't believe … I knew I should have never let her get a job!" she started sobbing.

"It's ok, Maggie. Is John there for you?"

"No, he's out of town for a bit," she said, choking on her tears.

"Do you have a friend who might be able to come sit … Maggie? Maggie?" And, the line went dead. *Dangit, unreliable cell service up here on the Rim.*

I looked around the campsite where Rod had apparently been camping this whole time. *Where is Isobel?* I felt slightly out of body right now, it was surreal that our quiet campground was now filled with rescuers. The police presence was quite large for this small community. I was surprised, and pleased, at the turnout.

Looking toward the west, the sun dipped lower in the sky, but still with plenty of daylight ahead. I could see that Greg was deep in conversation with another forest service ranger. I didn't see Charlie or Julie, so I decided to walk up to their campsite and see how I could help over there. When Shadow and I rounded the corner where we could see their camp, it was evident that the Search & Rescue volunteers were gathering there.

"Julie, what can I do?"

"Oh, Libby … isn't this terribly sad. Greg told me that this is the girl that you had come here looking for?" She reached out and gave me a big hug.

"Yes, it appears so. I think I'm still in shock because I really expected to find Isobel enjoying her days off with her friends. I can't believe she is *actually* missing."

"Well, let me introduce you to the Search & Rescue team. I'm sure there is something you can do to keep your mind occupied and not thinking of the worst."

Once all the volunteers had gathered, the lead man started in with what we knew and what we didn't know. The boyfriend was in custody, but not talking. "The young woman's cellphone was found on a ridge near forest road 188 and a K-9 team is already over there searching for any other evidence. A group needs to scour this campground, but we're waiting for the police to give the go ahead after they've thoroughly searched the site they're working now. Another group should start getting missing person posters up around the towns of Forest Lakes, Heber/Overgaard, Show Low, and Payson."

"Here's an enlargement of a recent photo of the young lady. Who volunteers to go get more printed and head up the task of getting them dispersed?" There were about twenty-five people who quickly raised their hands and jumped into action.

"Anyone good with computers and social media?" he called out.

A few ladies in the back raised their hands. "We're local and can start posting missing person notifications on all the social media bulletin boards."

"That's great … go ahead and get started on that, and thank you!"

I volunteered to head over to Heber/Overgaard with a group of five others and get posters up at as many businesses as possible.

* * *

Back at my campsite, I retrieved Trina and loaded Shadow in the back. As I was pulling out, Greg was driving up. I rolled down my window.

"Howdy!" he called out.

"Hey, just headed over to Heber to help distribute missing person posters."

"Mind if I tag along? It is still my day off and I'd love to help however I can," he asked.

"Sure, leave Whitey here and jump on in."

On the twenty-minute ride over to Heber, he filled me in on what the police were saying. "Apparently, Rod says Isobel never came camping with him and he didn't understand why everyone was getting so upset. We explained that her mother is looking for her and she is missing. That's about the time he decided to shut up and not talk anymore. They're holding him on felony counts of reckless endangerment by leaving his campfire going, evading officers, and speeding violations."

"Did he indicate why he was running?" I inquired.

"Not really, but after I talked to him about his campfire, I think that's why he told the cops as much as he did. I'm not real clear on that though."

"I really wish I could ask him why he specifically kept running from *me*. How does he even know who I am?" I added.

"Yeah, something doesn't add up, does it?"

We pulled into the library parking lot where everyone agreed to meet. One of the volunteers worked here and said the library would donate the free copies of the posters we were to hang around town. We grabbed our stack of posters, a stapler, and some tape and proceeded to the far end of town near the local bakery and decided we would work our way back to the library.

"While we're here, let's grab some donuts and coffee?" Greg offered.

"Well, we certainly have to support local business, so we might as well." *A man after my own heart.*

We bought a few dozen donuts and several large to-go carafes of coffee since we knew a lot of volunteers who would require a sugar and caffeine rush not long from now. That's a contribution we were very happy to make. It didn't take us long in this small town to get all our flyers hung; everyone was more than happy to participate and asked how they could get involved to help. Ah, I love small communities who pull together for the greater good. It's so heartwarming and such a refreshing change from the big city.

We left the donuts and coffee off at the library, and as we were leaving, I swear I saw scruffy John, Maggie's whatever, walking out of the hardware store across the street. *What is he doing here?* I stopped and watched the man load a bunch of stuff into the back end of his older style light brown Bronco and then get in and pull out onto Hwy

260 toward Show Low. *Hmm, that is strange. Did Maggie tell him to come up here to search for Isobel? I don't recall seeing him at the volunteer gathering earlier? Was this Bronco one of the many vehicles I saw parked at their house?*

"It's clear this direction, if that's what you're waiting for," Greg interrupted my thoughts.

"Oh, sorry, thought I saw someone I knew across the street there. Which is weird because I don't really know anyone here. I'm sure I'm mistaken."

All the way back to the campground, I couldn't stop thinking about the last couple calls with Maggie. There was something strange about the way she had reacted to me on the phone ever since I agreed to help out with her daughter. *Was it me? Am I losing my mind, or is she truly behaving differently?*

"Still leaving in the morning?" Greg asked.

"Yes, that's the plan. I sure hope they'll find Isobel soon. If not, I'll definitely be back to help." *And hoping to stare in those endless blue eyes some more? Libby, stop it!*

"Well, perhaps we can find some dinner tonight or grill something up at the campground?" he asked.

Oh, my ... he really is hitting on me, isn't he? Those eyes... that jawline ... those muscles. Look at the way his shirt fits so nicely ... LIBBY! Answer the question!

"Uh. Um. What?" That is seriously all I could conjure up.

"You seem distracted. Of course, your friend's daughter is missing; I'm being thoughtless, perhaps selfish, in wanting to spend more time with you. I understand."

"Oh, no ... no. Yes. Well, my mind *is* a bit scattered today, but I do have to eat this evening." I looked over my right shoulder to the back seat, "Shadow, want company for dinner?" She barked and started doing her happy dance.

"Ok, that settles it," he said, laughing.

* * *

The thing about camping in the middle of the forest, boondocking, there are no showers. What exactly was I thinking in inviting a man over to share my fire when I haven't showered in nearly two days? *At least you know what you will not be doing, Libby! That should take the pressure off.*

Shadow started barking and running toward the road. "Shadow! Stop! Get back here NOW!" She did. On a dime, she turned and came right back to me. I saw now what she was barking at ... looked like Charlie was on the move again in his putt-putt. He saw us and waved as he sped by. Not five minutes later, he was pulling in our campsite. "Shadow, stay. You stay right there." I got up and started walking toward Charlie.

"Looks like the coppers are gone now. Camp is all cleaned up. They took all of that hoodlum's stuff ... s'pose for evidence," Charlie informed me.

"Did the K-9 unit find anything else up on the ridge?" I asked, praying that something would further this investigation along.

"Dunno. The volunteer group is gatherin' again at our place tomorrow mornin' around eight. You joinin'?"

"I really wish I could, but I've got to get back to town for business. I plan on visiting the girl's mom, too," I said.

"Well, we'll miss ya' round these parts," he said, firing up his side-by-side and taking off.

Strange little man. That's all I could think of as he pulled away.

The sun was setting farther onto the horizon, painting golden strokes of wispy clouds across the remaining blue sky as though a serious artist had spent hours creating this work of art. Closing my eyes, I breathed in fresh air deep into my lungs and exhaled slow, long, and steady, releasing all of today's tensions out into the dusk. When I opened my eyes, the sky's tapestry had changed to an even more stunning deep red that took my breath away. *I don't want to go back to the city.*

Better get the fire going so we have some hot coals to cook on. Just as I maneuvered to do that, Greg pulled up. This is getting too comfortable and to think, I only met him last night.

"Hey, I found a great deal on some filets!" he shouted pulling several grocery bags from his backseat.

"Fantastic!"

"I realized at the store that I have no idea what your tastes are, or whether you even eat meat?" he said.

Laughing, I said, "Yes, I eat meat. Overall, I try to eat healthy, lots of fruits and veggies are the mainstay of my diet, but I do splurge on occasion. It's not like I eat steak several times a week or anything." The look that appeared on his face told me that's exactly what he does.

"Yeah, I'm a meat and potatoes type of guy. That's healthy, isn't it?"

"Well, you don't look like you're malnourished or weak, so I guess you're doing it right!"

We opened a bottle of wine while we waited for the fire to settle down into some useable coals. It was a nice evening, cool enough for a jacket, but pleasant to sit out. We talked and learned more about each other. Not only was he easy on the eyes, he was a great conversationalist too. After enjoying our nice, tender and juicy steaks, we must have talked for three more hours by the warm fire. Shadow had long since given up on us and was sleeping in the tent. I really didn't want to leave in the morning, but I had already made up my mind that I would be back here soon.

"I guess I better be getting home; it's late and I know you'll be up and out of here early," Greg said.

I sighed, probably a little louder than I planned. "I really don't want to go, but duty calls."

"Can I ask for your phone number? I've enjoyed our time together and, if it's not too forward, I'd really like to continue to get to know you." Hesitantly, he slowly raised his downcast eyes to meet mine.

Thank goodness for the dark, hopefully he wasn't seeing me blush.

"I'm uh, well ..." I struggled for the right words.

"Oh, it's ok. I shouldn't have asked. I'll get going. You travel safe tomorrow." He was already half way to his truck by the time I could get my words out.

"Wait!" I finally spoke up, and walked slowly toward his truck. "I'm not good at this."

How do I tell him that I screw up every relationship I've ever been in? He seems sweet, but this never works out well for me. I hadn't even entertained the idea of dating, or anything close to it, for so long now. *Libby, you don't even know that's what he wants. It never hurts to have more friends.*

He went to open his truck door, and I started again, "I've really enjoyed today; hiking, volunteering, this dinner, and talking for hours. I don't know what more I can give than that ... it's been a long time, and I just don't date well. I'm quite independent and not good at sharing my independence. But, I love the idea of talking and learning more about you and I do come up here fairly often so I'd love to go hiking again. Does that sound okay? For now?"

His eyes shined in the distant soft glow from the fire's remaining embers, and his smile was genuine. "I'd love to go hiking again."

"Hand me your phone so I can give you my digits." I held out my hand, he placed his phone in it. I typed my phone number into his contact list.

"Safe travels with Trina!" he said as he retrieved his phone, gently brushing against my hand.

"We'll do our best. It's the other crazies out there that worry me." I smiled and waved goodbye as he left our camp. *I'm never washing this hand again.*

I joined Shadow in the tent after securing everything back in Trina and making sure the fire was out. It had gotten much cooler, I thought, smiling. *Wonder why I hadn't noticed that sooner?*

Must have been the wine, but I was out cold once my head hit my pillow.

Suddenly, and groggily, I sat up. *What the hell was that?* Shadow barked and bared her teeth. *Crap, what is out there?* I could barely hold Shadow back and didn't want her barreling through the tent's screened door.

I grabbed my flashlight and pointed it out the door.

"Who's there?" I yelled.

I heard rustling of leaves, possibly twigs snapping. It sounded loud in the still of the night. *A bear? A coyote? Please tell me it's not a human!* I'm generally good with nature and much more afraid of human beings.

I snapped Shadow's bra and leash in place and carefully unzipped the tent. Still shining the flashlight around, and not seeing any eminent danger, Shadow's leash in my left hand and the spotlight in my right, we slowly crawled out of the tent.

As soon as I stood fully upright, Shadow bolted, barking her fully alert voice, and pulling the leash right out of my hand. I fell to the ground. *Dammit!*

"Shadow! SHADOW!!!! Get back here!!!" I screamed.

I had dropped the light when I fell and it was pitch black out. Scrambling around, I found it and shined it toward the forest. "SHADOW!!!" I screamed her name, again and again. I heard her barking still, so she wasn't that far away.

What the heck is that? I swiveled to the left so fast I nearly lost my balance. A large rustling sound came from the edge of the forest. Just then, in the shadows cast by my light, I distinctively saw a large person running. It wasn't close, maybe fifty yards away?

"Hey! Who's out there? SHADOW!!!"

From behind, something rushed toward me. Then, a loud crash, and darkness took over.

CHAPTER SIX

Libby, what the heck have you done now? You chased away gorgeous blue eyes … you didn't find Isobel … and now, you lost your sweet little girl.

Libby? Libby? Hey, Libby?

There were voices all around me. Was I making this up? Were these just my thoughts?

Get 'er some water.

A man's voice.

Then, a woman's voice.

If I knew what happened to her, don't you think I'd tell ya?

Light. There is light. Wait, wasn't it middle of the night? My eyes kept trying to open, but it felt like they were glued shut … a sandy, gritty feel to them.

She's comin' to! Libby? Hey, Libby?

I opened one eye only a sliver. It was light out.

Libby!

Charlie? What? Where am I?

Then, I got the biggest kiss right on my lips. "Ugh! What the ....?!" I opened my eyes full and found Shadow ready to wash the rest of my face. She was licking, and jumping around, and almost squeaking, she was so excited. I slowly moved to sit up and realized that I was incredibly stiff and sore.

"Libby! Oh, my goodness, we thought we'd lost you!" Julie exclaimed. "What on earth are you doing out here? What happened?"

I stared at her and then turned my head gently and fixed my gaze on Charlie. Still confused, and not fully understanding anything, I grabbed the water Julie offered. I sipped it for a bit while I continued to collect my thoughts. My stomach lurched. Maybe water will wait for later.

"I, uh, heard something. Something was out here. Shadow ran." I drank more water. *Think, think ... What happened, Libby?*

"I think I saw someone running, but it was so dark out." I looked over to Shadow, "Thank goodness you came back, I was so scared I lost you!" I hugged and loved on her for a few more moments.

"Well, we's woke up this mornin' hearin' some whinin' goin' on...." Charlie started, "I looked out the window and there's Shadow. I says to the missus, 'what on earth is Libby's dog doing over here?' and we decided to bring her back to ya."

"She went over to your place?" I asked, shocked.

"Yep, then we brought her here and found you passed out cold," he said, looking directly at the wine bottle that got left out near the fire pit. "Must have been some night." He winked.

"No, somebody was here. Someone hit me …" I felt the back of my head and winced. "Ouch! Yes, right here, I have a huge knot." I drank more water.

"I'mma gonna call the police," Julie said, pulling out her phone.

"What time is it?" I asked.

"It's about six," Charlie answered.

"Thanks. Can you hand me my phone from over there?" I asked, pointing toward the entrance to the tent.

"Hey there. Yep, still in the mountains. I'll be there a little later this morning than I thought. There was an incident last night. Oh, no, no… I'm fine. But, let's plan to meet up tomorrow instead, is that ok?" After reassuring Alexis several more times that I was okay, we hung up.

I looked up and saw Whitey speeding down the road and right into my campsite. Greg jumped out and ran over, wide-eyed, and clearly worried.

"What happened, Libby?" he asked.

I smiled as big as I could with my head still pounding. "How did you know to come here, the police haven't even arrived yet?"

"Police scanner. They're right behind me." And, that they were. Two state troopers pulled up.

I spent the next hour trying to recall everything I could remember, which wasn't a whole lot. I knew both Shadow and I heard something, and she took off running after whatever it was. I thought I saw a shadowy figure, but after that, I had no idea what happened to me other than having a bump on my head and a substantial headache now. I continued to drink water throughout this interrogation, and agreed to go with Greg to get some breakfast before I packed up camp and headed out. I think he wanted to be certain I was ok to drive, so he wanted to observe me for a while longer. Probably smart.

* * *

We chose an outdoor table on the patio at the café. After placing my order for a veggie omelet and wheat toast, and thoroughly enjoying my coffee, I asked Greg if he'd learned anything more from the police about my incident, or Isobel's disappearance.

"There hasn't been anything more, related to the girl," he answered.

"I'm stumped. Where would she be if she didn't go camping with Rod? And why did Maggie think she had gone camping with friends? She definitely didn't know about this boyfriend."

"I don't know, but one thing is for sure … they have an extensive team looking for her. It shouldn't be long before we know something."

"Who the heck was creeping around my campsite last night? I've been camping in these hills for over thirty years and have never had anyone come into my camp during the night. I wonder if it's related to Isobel's disappearance? We know Rod is still detained, so it wasn't him … but if not, then who?"

"Agreed, very disturbing. Nothing like that happens around here. And, the fact that they hit you over the head, but didn't steal anything from you, or kill you …" he shuttered visibly, "well, I can't explain the motive here. What did they want from you?"

"I know! Doesn't make sense. Ahhh, look at that omelet… thank you!" I turned toward our waitress and was drooling now over the bubbling hot cheesy omelet she delivered. "Can I please get more coffee, too? Thanks."

We quieted down for a bit as we enjoyed our nice, piping hot breakfast. I guess we were both hungry because we sure were focused on our plates.

"I'm extremely grateful you are doing as well as you're doing now. I have to say, I was in a state of panic when I heard over the scanner that there was a woman unconscious on forest road 171. I felt so helpless and felt propelled to get to you … God knows how many traffic laws I violated on my way, but the moment I saw you sitting up, I …" he choked up, then cleared his throat and sipped his coffee. "I finally could breathe, and I wanted to kill whoever harmed you."

"Wow. Kill?"

"Well, you know. It's how I felt in the moment. No, don't get me wrong. I'm not a killer!" We both chuckled and I reached out and took his hand.

"Thank you. I'm flattered you care and you dropped everything to come find me." I gave his hand a little squeeze and then reached for my coffee cup again.

"Feel good enough to drive back to Mesa today?" he asked.

"Yes, I'm feeling much better. Now that I've had food, I think I'll take some Advil for the headache. I'll be fine."

"Darn it! I was hoping you'd convalesce at my place for a few days," he teased.

Nearly choking on my mouthful of coffee, "Wha … what?"

"Ok, mostly, I'm kidding you … I know, don't rush things." Smiling, he grabbed the check and I just knew not to argue with him over it. He was being kind to me and I truly appreciated it.

Back at the campground, he helped me gather all my belongings and saw me on my way. As I drove the familiar route home, I found my mind wandering back to our time together, both last night and this morning. He seemed like a genuinely nice person. I really enjoyed the couple days in the mountains despite the drama that surrounded Isobel and Rod, and whatever it was that happened overnight. *What did happen overnight? Who was that out there? And, why me?*

I pulled up at my house off Thomas Rd around one in the afternoon. Shadow slept the whole way, but the second the garage door started opening, she sprung right up. Guess she's rested now. *I wonder where she was all night, and thankfully, no large wild animals got hold of her.* She bounded out of the 4-Runner and right to the garage entrance, waiting for me as I gathered a load of our stuff. *All I want is a nap.*

My phone started ringing, but my hands were so full I couldn't get to it. We got in and I threw everything in my arms onto the living room sofa and finished unloading the car before I checked my phone.

"Hi Maggie, you called?"

"Libby. Why … Why?" Maggie breathlessly said. Was she crying?

"Why what, Maggie?"

"The police called, questioning *me*. Why are they questioning *me*?" She cried, but it was more than that. She sounded breathless and almost as though she were slurring her words, too.

"Well, I assume they are trying to get more information to help with their investigation." I replied. "Listen, I just walked in the door. What about once I'm settled in more, I come over and we can talk? Do you need anything? I could bring dinner perhaps?"

Between sobs she said, "Ok. I don't have much of an appetite, but dinner does sound good. What time?"

"I'll be there around six, okay?"

Once that was all worked out, I hopped in the shower and let the warmth waterfall over my entire body. For several minutes I didn't even move, letting it caress and soothe everything that ached. Nothing feels as good as a nice hot shower after camping. Clean hair, scoured body, and the freshness felt for hours after getting out. Nothing else like it. The other comfort appreciated after crawling out of the hills, is my wonderful TempurPedic bed. I laid down and let every surface of my body melt into the mattress. Shadow crawled up next to me, so snuggly and warm; we were out for hours.

I jolted awake and saw that it was already 5:30 p.m. The last thing I wanted to do was leave the house, but I took Shadow out to the backyard and let her do her thing, poured kibble into her bowl, and told her I'd be right back. After stopping through the drive-thru at Boston Market, I called Maggie to tell her I was running a few minutes late, but I was on my way.

"I didn't even know they still had Boston Market in the area," she commented, as we both devoured warm sliced turkey breast, mashed potatoes, steamed vegetables, and delicious dinner rolls.

"I haven't had this in years, but saw it on the way and it seemed like great comfort food." *For both of us.*

"Other than the police interrogation, no one is really telling me anything."

"Are you sure Isobel went camping with friends?" I asked her.

"That's what she told me."

"Well, there are multiple agencies, including a large volunteer rescue force in Coconino County looking for Isobel. Is there anything else you could tell me about her or her friends?" I asked.

"I really don't know." She looked tired, but something was still off. She didn't appear as distraught as I imagined she was when I talked to her on the phone. In fact, she didn't even look like she'd been crying, but her color and her speech were off. Something wasn't right.

"Is John your husband?" I blurted it out, I needed to know.

"Nah. We've known each other a long time. I guess he's my boyfriend, but that sounds silly at my age." She waved off the subject like she didn't want to talk about it.

"I thought I saw him in Heber yesterday. Does he have business up there? Does he happen to drive an older Bronco?"

She got up and walked into the kitchen to throw her container away. I heard water running. It took her several seconds before she answered me and I was beginning to wonder whether she had heard me or not.

"He's in plumbing and yes, he travels a lot. I'm not sure where he is right now, though. Why all the questions, Libby? You're as bad as the police." She was clearly irritated now.

"Sorry. You sounded so upset earlier, and I hoped he was here for you."

"Well, thank you for bringing me dinner—I think it's best if you leave now."

And that was that. I left for home with an uneasy feeling in my gut.

* * *

After a great night's sleep, everything looked different to me. I got up early, took Shadow for a long walk around the neighborhood before the sun was up and the sidewalk got too hot for her paws. Even in late May, the heat is brutal once the sun comes up. When we got back from our walk, the coffee was done brewing and smelled heavenly. I had my typical two cups before I hit my yoga mat for a good thirty-minute workout. Just as I was done, my phone rang.

"Good morning, Alexis!" I'm sure I sounded much more chipper than yesterday morning.

"Hey, I'm getting little man fed and I'll need to bring him with me since daycare is closed. Meet you at the spa at 8:30?"

"Sounds perfect. See you then."

The drive to work is relatively short, exactly as I planned it when we decided to buy this building. Previous to opening this business, I used to drive over sixty miles round trip for work. Never again. Looks like Alexis beat me here, I saw her Lexus parked right in front. Other than her car, the entire parking lot was empty. The building we owned was at the far northwest end and separate from the rest of the strip center, but it was obvious all the businesses were shut down. The magnitude of the pandemic still hadn't fully sunk in for me, but I had a feeling reality was about to slap me in the face.

"Hiya!" I said as I walked through the door and

found Alexis sorting mail at the front counter. I could immediately smell that she started the teapot and steeped some wonderful vanilla cinnamon tea. I grabbed a cup immediately. "Hey, big guy ... you've grown so much since I saw you last!" I picked up her son, Joshua, and swung him around, set him back down, and watched him run off again. *Wow, such energy!*

She stopped what she was doing, smiled and walked over, gently embracing me into one of her famously comforting hugs. "How was your camping trip, love? Did you catch up with the girl you were looking for? Oh, and what 'incident' ... what happened?"

"Camping trip was great...uh, I mean, good." She immediately caught on to my tone, my grin.

"Wait, you met someone!" she teased with that sparkle in her beautiful deep brown eyes.

"Yes, and no ... let me finish! The weather was wonderful up there and I absolutely loved being outdoors— no surprise there, huh? I didn't find Isobel, unfortunately— but we did find her phone and, sadly, I'm coming around to the fact that she is indeed missing. I'm praying nothing *bad* has happened to her."

"Oh, no ... that is awful, poor girl. I hope they find her soon." She stopped, then gave me the teasing look again, "*And...?*"

"And, yes, I did meet a handsome forest service ranger. But no, it's not like that. He's really nice and all, but we all know how this will turn out. Mostly, we are just looking for a missing person, nothing more."

"Oh, c'mon, Libby. You are as capable of a relationship as anyone else and you know it. I thought my meditations were settling you down, allowing you to *find yourself?*"

I did love meditating with Alexis. She had a way of bringing me back to earth—I've never found anything else that works like her sessions.

"Of course they're working. I just need a lot more work!"

"You just need to trust yourself," she added.

I continued to fill her in on the dreamy blue eyes of Mr. Gorgeous and all the happenings that went on up north surrounding Isobel. Then, it was down to business. And not being able to open our business doors was definitely not helping.

"Listen, I have several clients that I've done mobile service for in the past, and who are calling me now wondering if I can continue. That's one way to continue bringing in some money," I suggested.

"True. That's how we started Dharma Inspired and we can certainly use it as a creative way to continue business. We have to be super careful, though—protocols for the virus, masks, testing, and not attracting attention from the authorities. I don't think they can actually prevent us from accepting an invitation from a client to enter their house, we don't need to advertise that we're still operating outside of our brick and mortar," she said.

"For the few clients who have already called me, I asked if they were willing to get a test a couple days before our appointment. They are willing. With that, plus mask wearing by both parties, I would be comfortable. Would you?" I asked Alexis.

"I think so. Are your clients living alone or have multiple people in the home?"

"Two of the ladies I talked to each live alone. No problem there. The gentleman who also asked about mobile service lives with his wife … I guess that means both would need to be tested. I'll run that by him. We definitely need to protect ourselves, and them."

"Ok, so that is one way to continue earning money until we can reopen the doors. What about pre-selling gift cards that could be used once things open up again?" she suggested.

We brainstormed many ideas and decided we'd be okay for several months. I was mainly worried about keeping our clients healthy and mobile. I had a couple who really depended on massage to keep them flexible enough to get around. Alexis wanted to be sure all clients returned at the end of all this and that we could still pay our mortgage on this building.

There was a knock at our door—we both looked up. It was JJ, Alexis' adoring husband, peering in the glass doors.

"Wow, that time passed quickly!" Alexis said as she glided over to the door, her flowing skirt and blouse billowing behind her. *She always looks like she's floating everywhere she goes—so graceful.*

"Hello, sweetie!" they embraced with a sensuous kiss, as though they just started dating and not like they'd been married eight years. *So jealous.* "Where's the little man? I'm ready to take him off your hands."

Then, he turned to me, "Hey Libby, how was camping?"

I got up to hug JJ. "So good to see you! It's been awhile. Camping was great." I noticed he was freshly showered, his short close-cut blonde hair was still a bit damp as we embraced and the side of head touched mine. He smelled great.

"She *met* someone…" Alexis interrupted.

"Oh? Do tell!" JJ teased.

"Nah, it's nothing. At least not yet. Stop it, Lex!" I protested, but then changed tone. "Hey, JJ ... could I ask a personal favor?" It just hit me that he's a police officer and maybe I could get a little more information about Maggie and scruffy John.

"Sure, Whatcha need?"

I explained the whole Isobel saga and that I don't trust this man Maggie is living with. I also told him about the scuffle in the forest.

"Geez, Libby...I didn't realize you were caught up in all that. Let me see what I can *legally* learn and pass along to you. I also have a buddy with the state police that I might be able to learn more from." I loved how he emphasized 'legally.' He has always been a *by the book* kind of man as long as I've known him.

"That would be fantastic, JJ. Thank you!"

"Daadddy!!!!!!" There was a flash past me and straight into his daddy's arms. *Sooo cute, this family.*

With that, I left them to talk and I headed to my therapy room. As soon as I walked in, I remembered the feelings I had last time I was in here. *Was finding that phone in those leaves a true premonition? Nah.* I gathered up some of my lotions, oils, sheets, and towels and threw them in a large canvas bag. Then I hefted my mobile table out of the closet, shut off the lights, and beelined it for Trina. I'm fairly strong, but holy cow, all this was heavy. Back in the building, I said my goodbyes to the Johnson family and set off for home.

* * *

You've gotta love the excitement that dogs exhibit the

second you walk through the front door. Whether you walked out to the mailbox for five seconds, or you've been gone hours, the way they wiggle, rub, and squeak always warms my heart. *I am loved!* Being a pup, Shadow wriggled and twisted as I let her out of her training crate and we headed straight outside, with her bumping into nearly everything along the way. Between squeals of delight, more bouncing, jumping, and then the sudden zoomies around our backyard, she could not control her excitement. *We've got to hit the trails and get more exercise ... clearly too much sitting around today.*

"Ok, ok ... we'll wait for it to cool down this evening and then we'll head out for a hike," I promised Shadow. She seemed to be satisfied with that. Well, that, and a treat for being such a good girl while I was away. My phone rang.

"Hi! Thank you for calling me back, Mr. Tinley. Yes, I am offering to bring my massage table to your home, if you are interested. We require that all household members be tested for the virus prior and wear a mask throughout the session. Is that something that you are interested in?" I asked.

After a resounding yes to being interested, I answered his questions, "Yes, of course, I will get tested prior and wear a mask as well. Is there anyone else staying with you at your home right now? No, ok. Well, if this is something you are comfortable doing, then I could get you on the schedule for Wednesday at 8 a.m. I know how you like the early mornings. Would that work for you?" We got everything sorted and I was just pleased to be able to work this week.

After following up with several of my other clients, I secured four more appointments for the week and managed to leave myself time to get back to the mountains in a few days, which would be perfect. I let Alexis know my plan and it sounded as though she was able to book several sessions as well. *Maybe the closure won't kill us after all?*

That evening, after a long hike with Shadow in the hills behind our housing development, I felt myself starting to get a bit antsy that I hadn't heard from Greg yet. Just as I was settling in to my evening routine, the phone rang, and the butterflies started fluttering again when I saw his name across my phone's display.

"Well, hello there, Mr. Lawson!" I answered.

"Ah, that is the voice I want to hear right about now. It's been one heck of a day!" he opened. "How is Libby doing down there in the valley?"

"Well, shutting our doors this week wasn't exactly fun, but I do think that Alexis and I have a good enough plan for managing. We're both going to do more mobile business for a bit." I started to shut down lights and get Shadow secured for the night. Time to hop in bed.

"Is that safe?" he inquired.

"Before we bought this building, it is how we operated. Of course, there are drawbacks to doing this, but all the clients I'll be seeing are long-time customers of mine so there is a level of trust already established. I think it will be fine."

"What about the virus?

"Yes, the whole world has changed, hasn't it? We definitely have a procedure in place for that as well," I sighed.

We chatted on for over an hour, and he filled me in on the progress of the search for Isobel. They were on day three of the search and nothing. No solid leads. And, Rod was still not talking.

The conversation then turned a bit more intimate as we continued to get to know each other. Both of us were eager to see the other again, and I promised as soon as my last massage was over on Thursday morning, Shadow and I would be on our way to the Rim again.

CHAPTER SEVEN

Thursday afternoon we were pulling up to the same campground we stayed at last week. Charlie was chopping some wood outside his trailer. I stopped and let Shadow out to run.

"Well, howdy, Libby! Wasn't expectin' ya back so soon!" he shouted out.

"Hey Charlie! How are things going?"

"Julie's in town with the group of volunteers. I'm cleaning up around here. Just got back from my rounds, cleaning up all these people's mess they leave!" He sounded irritated about the most recent campers.

I was heading over closer to the trailer where he was standing and noticed Shadow was really interested in something closer to Charlie's red side-by-side. He kept chopping wood, so I went on over to the dog.

"What are you getting into over here, Shadow?" She was sniffing as if someone dumped out bacon grease. I caught a glimmer of something shiny. Looking back at Charlie, he wasn't paying attention, his back was turned. I quickly picked up the shiny object—*a necklace*? It was a delicate, little butterfly and flower. It looked like it could have fallen off of Charlie's little buggy. *Doesn't look like anything Julie would wear? I'll just slip it in my pocket and ask her later.* He looked over and started heading our direction.

"Whatcha guys doin' over yonder?" he asked.

I tried to divert his attention. "Shadow smells something ... but I don't see anything so probably just a squirrel. Hey, any more on the search team and finding anything related to Isobel's disappearance?"

"Nah, nothin' that I know of. Maybe Julie will learn something today in town?"

"Well, just wanted to say hi. We're going to get set up again at our campsite ... it's open, isn't it?" I asked.

"Oh, yeah, everyone that was here over the weekend has pulled out now."

"Ok, we'll see you later then. C'mon Shadow, let's go!" After grabbing a leash and pulling her away, we finally got back in the car and headed down the road.

Shadow leaped from the car as soon as I opened the door, almost as though she remembered we had been here before. She ran all over, sniffing, then she came to 'help' me put up the tent. Every time I tried to secure a pole, I swear she'd just barrel right over me and the tent. Finally, I got it all set and unloaded the sleeping bag and ice chest from my vehicle when a truck pulled up. *Whitey!*

"Well, that was good timing! I just got done setting up camp," I yelled over to Greg as he got out of his Tundra.

"Ready for our hike?" he asked, excitedly.

"You bet. Let me grab my pack and some water. Oh, better bring treats for her majesty, too."

It felt like I hadn't left the mountains at all; we fell right back into comfortable conversation as we hiked near the same ridge where we'd found the phone previously. We didn't take the exact same route, but we wanted to check out that ranch house again to see if it looked like anyone had occupied it since we last were there. Maybe they'd seen something and could be of help in the investigation? I also took a mental note … maybe JJ could help research who owns this property and I could get a number and talk to them.

The afternoon was warmer but still mild, all things considered. When you leave one hundred plus temperatures in the valley, the high seventies and low eighties feel amazing. I was soaking up the fresh air and sunshine when I heard … *a cowbell?*

Yep, that was exactly what I heard. I grabbed Shadow before she realized what was going on. As I was clasping her leash, a sheep dog wandered by us about fifty feet away. *Good call, Libby… that was nearly a confrontation.*

"Ah, the sheep are not far behind, are they?" Greg noted. "I thought I heard the herder's cowbell, and it looks like I was right."

We watched a large flock of sheep saunter by, with their two white sheep-herding dogs closely guiding the way … one about mid-pack, and the other one heading up the rear.

"As long as you don't approach the sheep themselves, the dogs won't even know we're here. They are focused on their job. These herds pass through this area all summer long and are also found closer by me in Heber, too." Right as he said this, Shadow started barking and getting jumpy. The sheep dogs just kept doing their job, I suppose we were far enough away from them not to be a threat.

"*Hola!*" a voice from behind us bellowed. We turned.

"Oh hi! This your flock?" Greg asked, pointing toward the sheep.

"*Si!*"

I had a thought, "Do you happen to know who owns the ranch just up beyond the ridge?" He stared at me like I was from Mars. Utter confusion.

"No hablo inglés," he replied, still looking confused.

I knew Spanish about as well as the sheepherder spoke English, and Greg wasn't much help either, but we fumbled our way using the basic schooling we did have, and gesticulating wildly as though we were the charades champions of the year.

Shortly after, as we continued our hike and Jurgi, the sheepherder, was long out of earshot, we busted out laughing.

"So glad no one saw how clumsy we were, trying to speak to that poor man!" I laughed out loud. "That was embarrassing. Guess I need to study up on my Spanish."

"I know! Did you see his face? I guess he knew we were talking about the sheep when I pointed to them, but after that ... he knew *nothing* we said."

"Well, he understood when you asked his name. We at least know it's Jurgi Salazar now," I added.

"I'm just glad he accepted our offer of water and some fruit. He looked exhausted, and so did his dogs." Greg grabbed a water for each of us and we continued our hike and enjoying the beautiful day. We could still see the sheep and their dogs way ahead of us now, but lost sight of the herder. Shadow was more settled the farther they traveled away from us and she walked right alongside of us now, off leash.

We approached the ranch house and again, we didn't see any vehicles or signs of life around the ranch.

"Do you suppose it's truly abandoned?" I asked Greg.

"I really don't know much about this place, but it sure looks that way."

Just then, there was a loud clatter and we all jumped, including Shadow. It sounded as though it came from the house, but it was so hard to determine. I leashed Shadow again, just in case. We proceeded to walk toward the large, wooden structure, heading toward the front door. Greg was calling out our approach to be sure we didn't surprise someone with a shotgun. The closer we got, and with no further sounds or sign of life, I began to question that the noise came from this direction. I kept looking from side to side, and behind me, as we approached though. *Am I the only one spooked by all this; Greg seems so calm!*

We peeked into the glass window that ran along the side of the large, worn cedar door. There was an iron doorknocker in the shape of a horseshoe right in the middle of the enormous door. I went to lift it to knock and was surprised at its weight. Using both hands, I lifted and let it fall to the door several times, where it made loud clanging sounds. *Well, if anyone is here, they certainly heard that!*

No one came to the door. No sounds that we could hear inside. So, we proceeded around the perimeter of the house, looking into windows along the way. Most of them were covered, but there were a couple smaller windows we could peer into. Shadow's sniffer was in full gear, all the way around the house. She was *very* interested.

"Here give me a boost ..." I said to Greg. There was a window slightly higher than my five-foot seven. I stepped one foot into the makeshift stirrup that Greg made with his fingers laced together. With one hand on his shoulder, I pressed to standing straight up and could see directly into a bathroom, and farther in, I could see a hallway. Right then, something moved inside. "Whoa! Something is in there!" I whispered, but leaned down to not be seen. Shadow let out a bark.

"What? Like a person or a critter?" Greg quietly asked, as I stepped out of his hands.

"Shadow, quiet!" I firmly but quietly scolded my dog, who continued to bark. "It seemed larger than a critter. Can you see in?" he was taller, and could see inside by standing on the tips of his toes. He stood there for a bit, while I watched out all around us.

"I don't see anything," he said. "Where did you see ... in the bathroom, or in the hallway?

"Hallway," I whispered back. "Shadow, get back here! Now!" She sidled up next to me and quieted down a little.

"Hmmm. Nope, nothing. Let's try the front door again."

We waited again at the front door, knocking several times with the heavy horseshoe. No one ever came.

"Well, it's not like we can break in, so if no one is here, then it is what it is. Let's go." Greg concluded.

"Can we check out that barn over there?" I pointed to the left of the house, and slightly up a hill where there stood a large red barn. Shadow appeared to like that idea, she started bouncing in that way that says, *Mom, let's go, let's RUN!*

"I guess. Do you really think this has anything to do

with Isobel's disappearance though?" he asked

"I'm not sure. I have this feeling and I guess since this is the closest homestead to where we found her cellphone, it seems like we should check it out. Don't you think?"

"I suppose. I'm just uncomfortable not being invited here."

"Yeah, I get it, let's call out our approach as we head up the hill and see what we see. It looks like the barn door may be open?" *I think it was actually falling off, the whole thing looks like it hasn't had maintenance this century.* Shadow was already running ahead of us.

The barn door was slightly ajar, we widened it a tad to squeak through. I mean, I would call this an open door … *no breaking and entering going on here. Ok, maybe the entering part, but still, we're just looking for the owner.* Shadow wasn't shy, she ran on in, with a full-on bark to announce our arrival.

Greg and I followed her in and stopped just inside the door to allow our eyes to adjust to the dark open space. *Where did Shadow disappear to, her black coat vanished within the darkness.* Looking up, small beams of light were streaming through high up … it was a loft with a bunch of hay. Once our eyes adjusted, we could see that the inside of the barn appeared pretty typical, there were tools, horse gear and tack, barrels, and feed bags spread around. There another door toward the back of the barn and it appeared to be open as well, I could feel the breeze drifting all the way through.

"I don't see Shadow. She may have run right through that door back there, so I'm going to check that out. Doesn't look like anyone is in here though, does it?" I said, walking through to the other exit.

"Shadow!" I should have had her on leash so I was

definitely kicking myself. I get so used to her being good and sticking by me, but she is just a puppy. "Shadow!" I called again. I heard some rustling, and out came my gangly long-legged girl bounding over as happy as I've ever seen her. Right then, I heard more rustling. *What the heck?*

"Greg, come here, hurry!"

I could see something in the tree line, but couldn't quite make out what it was. Greg came up beside me, breathing heavily. "What's wrong?"

"There's something, or someone, in the trees ... right over there. Do you see?" He started walking closer to see better and at that moment, one lonely sheep came out of the forest. Greg turned to look at me and I saw Jurgi, the sheepherder taking off in the other direction, deeper into the forest.

"Look!" I cried out, "Jurgi's running away from us!"

* * *

"This sure wasn't the hike I thought we'd be taking today," Greg stated, back at camp now.

"I'm not making sense of any of it. Why was the sheepherder at the abandoned ranch in the first place?"

"Maybe he wanted a spot to rest for a bit and he bedded down in the barn? I mean, for all we know, he has an agreement with the owner to use the barn?" Greg answered.

"I don't know, something smells fishy to me." It was right then that I remembered the small dainty necklace that I put in my cargo shorts pocket earlier. I pulled it out and started examining it.

"What's that?" Greg asked.

"A necklace I found under Charlie and Julie's side-by-side when I stopped in there earlier to say hi." I was turning the metallic butterfly/flower over to see if there was an engraving or anything that might be distinguishable.

"Maybe it's Julie's?" he asked.

"Yeah, maybe." I truly didn't think it was. This was quite girly for someone as rugged as Julie. I never saw her wear any jewelry either; it didn't seem like her. I pulled out my phone and snapped a picture of it. Then I texted Maggie and asked her if she recognized it. Something told me it was jewelry a younger girl, even twenty-something, would wear.

"Thanks for the hike today, though, it was still great exercise—beautiful scenery and Shadow sure loved it." We both glanced over to where she was conked out on her doggy bed. Completely out. Done for the day.

"I wonder if we actually learned anything more about Isobel's whereabouts today?" Greg asked as he got up and grabbed a bottle of water from the ice chest. "Want one?"

"Sure, throw me one, thanks!" *Why did I tell him to do that? I can't catch anything thrown to me!* I thought as I went over backward trying to grab the bottle hurtling through the air. *Ow, that hurt!*

Greg just laughed. "Sorry! I thought since you asked me to throw, you'd catch it!" he continued laughing, holding a hand out to me and helping me up as I grimaced.

"Not sure what I was thinking … ugh!" I said, breathlessly.

In order to stop laughing, I think, he cleared his throat and then continued on the subject of Isobel. "So, here's what we know … Rod says she never went camping with him, no one has seen her around here, including camping with Rod; we found her cellphone on the ridge nearby where the ranch is; there's a necklace that could be anyone's—doesn't really mean anything; there's a sheepherder who doesn't speak any English and *possibly* was in the barn at the ranch and *possibly* ran from us."

"And don't forget Maggie's boyfriend ... I don't trust him as far as I can throw him! According to Maggie, he hasn't been home, I think since Isobel's disappearance, and I'm sure I saw him coming out of the hardware store in Heber last week," I added.

"I guess I didn't know about this man?"

"I might not have mentioned it, but he sure gave me the willies when I first met him at their house. And Maggie got weird when I started asking about him, too."

We both looked up at the same time. Julie was pulling into my campsite in the beat-up old Ford. "Howdy!" she yelled, hanging out the window. She parked and walked over to where we were seated.

"Hey, anything new from Search and Rescue?" I inquired.

"I wish there were, but everyone is gettin' impatient since there's not been even one sightin' of this girl. I mean, do we even know she was ever up in these hills?"

"I think we are all getting to that point where we're questioning everything we've been told. Except, I keep going back to wondering how her cellphone got where we found it. I think that proves she was in this area," Greg added.

"True, true..." Julie said.

"Julie, does this belong to you?" I pulled the necklace out and handed it to her.

She quickly replied, "I don't wear any of that shit ...

are you kiddin' me?'"

I laughed because that was exactly what I thought she'd say. *So, why was it found near their side by side? Hadn't Charlie said he'd just finished cleaning campsites—he would have come back in that vehicle? Wonder where he picked this up from?*

My phone was ringing and I left the two talking so I could hear.

"Libby? I have something." It was Alexis' husband.

"Yes, JJ, whatcha got?"

"So, I did some preliminary searches online related to Margaret Crenshaw and I thought you'd find this interesting. Child Protective Services has been called out to her address multiple times over a fifteen-year period. Reports to CPS were called in citing child neglect."

"*What?* Maggie? That can't be right." I was stunned.

"More interesting, there are absolutely no arrests on her record. I don't find any evidence that she was taken in or Isobel was removed from the household," he continued.

"Ok. Maybe some disgruntled neighbors, or friends that became enemies? Who would call CPS on someone they know that *isn't* abusing their child? Seems like *someone* saw *something* they didn't like."

"No idea. I'm going to dig a little deeper and try to determine who called these in. Not sure I'll be able to get to that information because of privacy laws and, you know, whoever did probably wants to remain anonymous for obvious reasons. I will give you a call as soon as I learn any more. I wouldn't confront Margaret with this information. Not yet, anyway." After asking me how everything was going at my end, we hung up.

Julie had left by then and Greg was on the ground rubbing Shadow's tummy, and she was thoroughly enjoying every single moment of it. I just stood there, briefly taking in the moment. The largest smile broke out across my face, and settled in my heart. *I'm so blessed.*

CHAPTER EIGHT

I heard the light pitter-patter of rain on my tent during the night, and I swear that made me sleep more soundly. The fresh rain-scented air makes everything smell better … the pines, the oak, even the dirt. I was laying there in the early hours of dawn recalling strange dreams I had during the night, and not really wanting to get up, but knowing I needed to pee. It was cool out, I wouldn't say *cold*, but I still didn't want to get out of my nice warm sleeping bag either.

I just lay there, thinking of that dream. *There was a girl in the hospital. A phone rang and I answered it. A sheep ran by.* Ok, doesn't make any sense whatsoever, I gotta pee! I got up, which then got Shadow stirring, too. I put some shoes and a jacket on and then went to the car for the toilet paper. Shadow was already done doing her thing by the time I was ready to walk down the road toward the vault toilets the forest service maintained. *Does Greg maintain these? I never asked much about his job. I'll have to ask. They don't smell horrible so whoever is cleaning is doing something right.*

On the way back from the outhouse, we took a longer walk around the whole campground. Well, I walked, Shadow ran ... from this side of the road to the other, continuously crossing in front of me trying to decide which side smelled better, I guess.

Hey, wait a minute. There are the sheep.

To our right, as we were heading back to our own camp, but maybe half a mile away from ours, I spotted a small old tiny camper, no truck to pull it. Lying around, all over the camp, were the sheep. I noticed the dogs too, and quickly snapped Shadow's leash on. *I didn't know he was camping here. How long? I'll have to ask Charlie.*

I heard a truck coming up the road, still a distance away, and for reasons unknown to me, I instinctively ducked into the forest to not be seen. I was across the road from Jurgi's camp, but hidden by thick forest. Ducking behind more brush, I kept a tight rein on Shadow and luckily, she followed my lead and seemed to also be 'hiding'.

The Bronco.
John?
John and Jurgi?
What the freakin' flip?

* * *

Shadow and I lurked quietly in the forest, watching the two men get out of the Bronco and walk up to the small run-down trailer. *I wish I could hear what they are saying.*

"Greg, are you working today?" I had moved deeper into the forest to make the call, and then paralleled the road almost all the way to where I could then come out of the forest, cross the road, and walk back into my camp. No one appeared to notice. Extremely surprising since Shadow isn't quiet at doing anything.

"Yup, I'll be done around 1:30, why?" he asked.

"I just saw the strangest thing. I was hoping you could come out here, but no worries, we can catch up later."

"Are you safe, Libby?" He sounded worried all of sudden.

"Um, yeah." Then with more certainty in my voice, "Yes, no worries. Sorry to call while you're working. I can fill you in later." Reluctantly, we hung up and I poured myself a cup of coffee.

"Oh, my sweet girl … you were such a good hide-and-seek player! Yes, you were!" I rubbed her ears and head, and she wiggled and made cute groaning noises.

Everything in me screamed to head back over that direction and see if I could catch any part of their conversation. *Maybe I could leave Shadow in Trina with windows cracked? No, go with your gut feeling … you don't need to get entangled with those guys, stay out of it!*

Forget common sense, I'm not good with patience or leaving things alone. I wish I was, trust me. Shadow was locked away in the vehicle, for just a few minutes. I headed through the forest on my side of the road now and tried to approach the sheepherder's camp from the back side this time.

Voices were raised, apparently the conversation wasn't going all that well.

"What do you mean? *Who* was at the ranch?" Scruffy John was saying to Jurgi.

"Some forest service guy and a woman with red hair,

beautiful eyes," Jurgi responded. *In English … he does speak English! I can't believe…*

"What did they see?"

"I have no idea … I ran!" Jurgi's hands swept out in front of him, pointing somewhere far away.

"You keep them away from the ranch, do you hear me?" John screamed, then stomped over to his Bronco and sped away.

I moved back, then tripped and fell. The rustling caught Jurgi's attention … and his dogs. I got up and ran all the way back to my camp. *Do they know I'm camping here at this campground? I've really gotta get out of here.*

* * *

I nearly had everything packed up when Greg pulled up.

"Hey, where are you going? Back to the city?" he said as he approached my vehicle.

"Long story. Wanna head into town for lunch and I'll tell you all about it?" I asked.

"Sounds like a plan. Wanna ride with me?" Greg asked hopefully.

"I'll meet you there. Wait, where? The Café?"

"Sounds great, meet you there."

When we pulled up, there wasn't another car in the lot. *I hope they're open.* I got Shadow out of the backseat, hoping they'll allow her on the patio.

We took a seat and one of the wait staff came out to get our drink order. She introduced herself and brought Shadow a little bowl of water, too, which without saying the words indicated my girl was welcome here.

"Thank you, Louise, I appreciate that!" I said as she loved on Shadow a little bit more.

"So, you sounded a bit concerned earlier when you called, and then I show up and you're all packed and ready to drive out? What's going on, Libby?" Greg asked.

"Remember I told you about Maggie's boyfriend … he gives me strange vibes?"

"Yeah, of course, I remember. The Bronco driver, right?"

"Yep. Well guess who he knows?" Greg's eyebrows lifted along with his shoulders, questioningly. "He drove the sheepherder back to his campsite this morning and I overheard them talking. Something about seeing us at the ranch." Louise set down my iced tea and Greg's water, then walked away, before I continued.

"I distinctly heard, '*keep them away from the ranch*'. That has to be about us, right? And, how do these two even know each other? Don't you find this extremely coincidental when we are looking for John's girlfriend's daughter?" I was loud-whispering now, trying not to let Louise hear the content as she kept coming over to our table.

This time she delivered my hot and cheesy pork enchiladas smothered in red sauce. They looked delicious. Greg ordered a cheeseburger and fries, which looked really good right now too. I guess I was hungry.

Greg took a bite of his burger and after he chewed and swallowed, he finally answered, "Wow. Yes. I don't know what to think, really. But, yes, it feels all very connected. Odd. Did they see you? Why did you pack up your camp?"

"I started to feel extremely uncomfortable being alone there. I do think Jurgi heard me in the trees, but I don't think he could have seen me. But, it doesn't take a rocket scientist to figure out that the gray 4-Runner at my camp is the same one I drove over to John and Maggie's so if those two get talking, they'll figure out it's me. I don't know what's going on here, but every instinct in me said to pack up and move."

"Where are you moving to?" Greg inquired.

"That's just it, I'm not sure. I feel like there is more to learn, and I need to be here to observe and perhaps talk to some others, too. But, then again, these guys know this area and they are going to see my 4-Runner no matter where I set up camp. John seems to know I'm here to find Isobel. Is he here to run me off? Why *is* he here? That's what I'd like to know." I felt my irritation level increasing.

"I don't want to be too forward here, but why don't you come to Heber and stay with me. I have plenty of space and they don't know where I live so you should be safe there." He looked at me in a cautiously optimistic way that made me smile.

"Careful what you wish for, buddy!" I teased. *Oh, boy... what am I getting myself into here? Libby, just go back to town.*

"Listen, I know what you're thinking, and I promise you I will make no moves whatsoever. I'm just a friend trying to help a friend out. That's it. I have plenty of room—you and Shadow will have your own space. No funny business, I promise. Unless, you want funny business and then we can negotiate." He laughed.

"What are your days off this week?" I asked.

"I actually have the weekend off, so I'm all yours until Monday. When were you planning on heading back to the city?" he countered.

"I have an appointment on Tuesday, so I thought I'd head back on Monday afternoon," I answered. "But, I was asking you that because *maybe* you'd want to camp with me. We could move across the highway to another campground to not be seen. What do you think?"

"That actually sounds fun, I haven't camped out in quite some time myself. But, don't you think the best way to keep an eye on Jurgi or John would be to stay right where you were camping? Or, maybe closer to Charlie and Julie?"

"I suppose you're right. And, if you were there with me, I'd feel a little more comfortable sleeping at night. You have a tent, don't you?" I asked.

"Actually, I'm not sure I still do, but I was thinking I could bring my RV over and park it instead. What do you think?"

"Sounds like a plan!"

We finished eating our food and each paid for our meals separately. I agreed I'd return to the campground, but move to the campsite that was in sight of our camp hosts. Greg headed back to his place to pack up and bring the RV over. We'd see each other again around dinner time, and we'd already decided to have no meal after this huge one. He was going to bring a bottle of wine and if we got hungry, we'd snack on cheese, crackers, and fruit instead.

Thankfully, the campsite was still open. It was getting later in the afternoon on a Friday so I was started to wonder. As I was pulling in, my phone rang through the speakers in my vehicle. I punched the button on my steering wheel to answer.

"Libby! Where did you find that necklace?" It was Maggie, sounding panicked.

"At a campsite nearby. Why? Do you recognize it?"

"Yes! It's Isobel's!" she cried.

CHAPTER NINE

A cool breeze whispered across my flesh sending a graduating shiver up my arms, over my neck, and straight through to my scalp. I moved closer to the fire and gazed into the flames that licked the edges of my already too browned marshmallow. Blowing quickly to put out the blue flame that torched it and using the graham crackers, I gently removed the sticky, gooey sweetness from the skewer by sandwiching it together along with half of a Hershey's chocolate bar.

"Sure looks like you're enjoying your dessert," Greg said, breaking into my mindful s'mores making.

I almost forgot he was still sitting there, this is how involved I get when I've decided to indulge in one of the best desserts we campers look forward to. Swallowing that bite, and taking another sip of wine, I smiled, "You don't want one?"

"Nah, not really my thing."

Really? Maybe I need to rethink his gorgeousness?

"Good. More for me." I loaded up another skewer with two more marshmallows and poured myself more Pinot Noir. "I've gotta say … I haven't tried s'mores with red wine before. This is my new favorite."

We both turned at the same time to look toward the road. Shadow jumped up from her position at my feet and was immediately on point, but she didn't bark. Her ears raised; her head tilted aside as though she was listening too.

"What *was* that?" Greg whispered as he stood up.

"Someone's arguing."

"Where is that coming from?" He started walking toward the road.

I hurried and swallowed down the last of my s'more with more red wine, grabbed Shadow's leash, a flashlight, and we joined Greg where the pullout to our campsite met the road.

"Sounds like a heated argument, let's go see who it is." Greg started walking much faster. Shadow and I followed; I wasn't so sure we should get involved in this. However, he is a ranger so I suppose it is his job to get involved.

"Greg! Watch it!" I yelled, as I realized a vehicle was approaching at the bend in the road ahead at a high rate of speed.

We both turned away from the plume of dust that flew up at us as it passed.

We started running now toward the next camp. Greg yelled back to me, "Did you see what type of vehicle that was?"

Breathing heavily, I tried to answer and still run. "I, I'm, pretty sure I saw … a Ford emblem, but it was difficult to see ... thr-through all the dust."

As we approached, we realized it was the sheep herder's camp. His dogs let out a warning bark and I realized I would not be able to enter with Shadow in tow. Greg moved ahead cautiously.

"Hello! Is everything ok here?" he shouted, then ran, calling over his shoulder to me, "The sheep herder! He's unconscious."

"I'm going to take Shadow back to the camp and I'll get the car so we can go get medical help." My sweet girl sure knows when something is urgent, we ran back to our camp like a life depended on it.

Pulling into the sheep camp, my headlights revealed that the herder was conscious again. They were seated on the ground now, and Greg looked like he was talking him into drinking some water.

"What happened?" I asked as I approached them.

"The best I understood was that his friend Juan was here for a meal," Greg said.

"Well, his face is sure bashed in, that was one heck of a 'meal with a friend'."

Jurgi was facing me now. "Juan es mi hermano," he said with a low croaky voice.

"Brother?" I asked. He understood and nodded. "Que paso?" I asked, touching my face and wanting to know what happened to his.

"Eh, nada." He waved his hand dismissing my question about what they were fighting over.

I found it hard to believe that someone gets punched over *nothing* and that's exactly the look I gave him. He wasn't having anymore of the inquisition and he certainly did not accept our offer to take him to urgent care so I tried changing the subject a bit.

"Rancho … esta manana?" I started off in broken remedial Spanish when all of sudden I remembered that I'd heard him speaking English with John when I was spying on them through the forest. "You were at the ranch earlier, we saw you. Why did you run away from us?"

His eyes got huge. *Ah, ha! He does understand me!*

"No sé."

Greg lost patience and grabbed him by his shirt. "That's a bunch of bull! You understood exactly what she said right now! Were you following us?"

"No, no…" Jurgi looked shaken. "Juan invited me there. I didn't know anyone would be there so I got scared."

"Why? What are you hiding?"

"Nada."

"Bullshit!" Greg jerked him closer.

"Ok, ok. Juan told me to make sure no one sees me there."

"Why? Who owns that ranch?"

"Juan owns it and I have no idea who he thought would see me. I was there to pick up some equipment from the barn that I needed."

"What do you know about the missing girl?" I threw out there.

The startled and blank expression on his face told me that he had no idea what I was talking about. We were done here for tonight.

* * *

Despite it being a late one the night before, Shadow and I were up before dawn and headed out for a walk so we wouldn't wake Greg, still asleep in his RV. I noticed there was no sign of life yet at our camp host's site either. It was clear that Shadow was much more interested in running this morning, so I let her lead me jogging down the road.

Well, we must have scared off Jurgi... I thought as we passed by his place. The herder, his sheep, and the dogs were nowhere to be seen, and the small camper was all shut up tight and looking abandoned. *They got an early start.*

We made great time running to the end of the three-mile road. There were quite a few new camps that had set up since we arrived the other day. Mostly families, and no one was awake this early. *I wonder if anyone else heard the dispute at the shepherd's place?*

I stopped to stretch the legs a bit and was prepared to walk back, but Shadow was still full of energy so we set off running for the return to camp. The sun was getting closer to breaking over the horizon; our breath puffed as if Shadow and I exhaled smoke. *Maybe this is actually proof of my dragon's breath from not brushing beforehand? Definitely can't start talking to Greg until I brush my teeth!*

As we ran up to camp, out of breath and ready for coffee, my eyes took in the scene: a handsome man rubbing his hands together over a fire he had just started and the smell of coffee on the camp stove. *I could get used to this.*

"Good morning!" I said as I ran right past him and straight to the tent to get that toothbrush.

"You two were sure up early it looks like?"

"Yeah, restless energy I suppose. We ran to the end of the road and back," I got in before starting on scouring the teeth.

"Wow, that's ambitious considering the late-night drama we had last night." He poured us both a cup of coffee.

"Ah, nothing better than coffee and toothpaste." I

cringed on the first sip.

"I need to get to the ranger station this morning and report the fight from last night. They like to keep that on record in case there are repeat occurrences. Since Jurgi wouldn't really tell us much, I'm not sure anything will actually be done. At least I will have done the obligatory paperwork though."

"What did you think about all that with Jurgi last night? And, what about his friend Juan owning that ranch?" I asked.

"With friends like that, who needs enemies?"

"Exactly. Wonder what specifically they were fighting about?"

"Probably a woman. Isn't that why most men fight?"

I thought about that for a second and honestly didn't know. "I swear it was a Bronco that threw dust all over us. But, maybe not. I guess I talked myself into believing I saw a Ford emblem. Wonder where Charlie was last night?"

"You know, we didn't see his truck come back last night before all that happened, did we?" Greg stood to get a better look over at their campsite. "Nope, it's still not there. Maybe those two went to the big city for a couple days?"

"Let's grab breakfast in town?" I suggested as I made my way to the tent to get changed.

"As long as we can get in a good hike later?"

"Deal!"

* * *

Piping hot French toast, two scrambled eggs, and a side of bacon was set down in front of me while Greg was admiring the huge breakfast burrito that he was about to receive.

"Can I get you two anything else? More coffee?" our waitress asked in a southern drawl that didn't quite sound to be from these parts.

"Could I get some Cholula for my eggs? And yes, more coffee please," I answered. Greg was already digging into his burrito as the waitress hurried off.

After devouring my eggs, I poured warm maple syrup over the French toast and took another bite of crispy bacon. "How long do you think you'll need at the station?" I asked as I wiped my mouth with a napkin.

"Maybe fifteen minutes? Twenty at the most."

"Ok. Would you be able to drop me off at the library and then pick me up on the way back?"

"Sure. Whatcha gonna do there?"

"Thought I'd try looking up local history on some of the properties around here. Namely, the ranch property that Juan might own, if we can believe Jurgi."

"Of course. I'll join you there when I'm done filing my paperwork."

We paid the bill, dividing it between us, and then headed out. I realized only after we pulled out of the restaurant parking lot that I could have walked to the library. It was silly that I hadn't ... Heber was a small town.

I held the door open for an elderly couple that was coming out of the library and then ran smack dab into one of the volunteers from Search & Rescue.

"Sorry!" the young lady fumbled as she stashed her phone in her pocket. "I really should be looking where I'm going."

"Hey, no problem. How's the search for Isobel going? Any new leads?" I asked.

"Most of the volunteers had to get back to their day jobs, but there are a few of us still working it. I'm surprised you're still here."

"Well, I did go back to the city for work for about a week and now I'm back. Staying over off 171."

"Oh." Her eyes looking down, and her body language sending signals to me that she was uncomfortable all of a sudden. "We were assigned over there the day…"

After a few more hems and haws, and clearly wanting to share something else with me, I prompted, "What is it? You seem bothered by something."

"Well, you know … uh, do you remember that scrawny guy, blonde hair, blue eyes, and has nappy hair? Uh, the one … he rides around on that red side by side—seems to be in charge. All the volunteers met at his campsite the first day?" Her eyes still downcast and wouldn't meet mine.

"Charlie?" I asked.

She looked up. I saw what I could only describe as fear in her eyes. I quickly turned around as she pushed past me and saw that Greg was entering the library. *What was that about? Is she afraid of Greg? Charlie?* I ran after her, but she was long gone.

"She was sure in a hurry. I saw you two talking--do you know her?" Greg asked as I was walking back to the front doors.

Still unsure of what I saw and what was going on, I decided to stay vague.

"She's part of the Search & Rescue volunteers, but I don't know her name. We were just talking about the search and she remembered somewhere she had to be."

"Are you ready? Did you find what you're looking for here?" he asked.

"No, I never made it that far, but it's okay, I'm really not sure I would have learned much here anyway. I'm ready to get back and see how much damage Shadow has done to your tenement on wheels." I smiled devilishly at him.

"Wait, isn't that the girl you were speaking to?" Greg asked as we were about to pull out of the library parking lot.

Looking across the street and down an incline into what appeared to be school grounds, I saw who he was referring to. *That's her all right, but who is that with her?* There were a few bushes blocking my view so I kept staring trying to determine who was with her. Finally, Greg said, "Isn't that Charlie with her? They must still be workin' the search."

That is Charlie. What the ... My instincts took over and I asked, "Can we drive over there? I have a question for them." I tried to remain as calm as possible so as not to alert Greg that there was any concern.

As soon as we pulled out of the library parking, and turned right to head to the school's parking lot, they both took off in separate directions. Charlie's Ford pickup was parked maybe a hundred feet away and he got there quick and sped off in the opposite direction. The girl ran, heading north into a neighborhood nearby. We couldn't get turned around quickly enough before we lost sight of both.

"Okay that was weird. Do you think they saw us?" Greg asked me.

Of course they saw us! Out loud I answered, "No, they must not have. That was a bit strange though ... both seemed in a hurry." *What's Charlie doing with the volunteer girl?*

* * *

We headed back to camp, rounded up Shadow who thankfully did not destroy Greg's RV while we left her to her own devices. She was a good girl so she got lots of loving and a few cookies before we headed out for our hike.

"What outdoor adventure do we want to seek today?" Greg asked.

"Let's head over to Chevelon Canyon Lake, what do you think?"

"Ohhh, I haven't been there in years. That's a great hike to get to the lake, but it's long. We should pack us up some sandwiches and make it a day."

It was the first time I had really seen inside his RV since he pulled it into my campsite yesterday late afternoon. I stepped in and was immediately drawn to how large it felt inside with the two slide outs. To my left, there was a dark brown leather sofa, then the kitchen area—not huge, but functional. It also had a nice dining table and what looked to be plenty of storage space. I was pleasantly surprised.

"I've never been in an RV this nice before," I said, looking around. "You could live in this thing ... it has all the comforts of home."

"That's the idea! Someday I'll get to retire and then I'd love to travel this nation of ours and live the great adventure."

My heart leaped. *Adventure ... travel.*

He must have seen the look on my face. "Is that something you've ever thought of doing?"

"It's really the only thing that drives me in life—travel and seeking new adventures. I can only dream of the day I could do it more frequently. And in a *home on wheels* ... how nice would that be? Never considered that. I've roughed it so far in all my outdoor adventures."

He just smiled and continued to get out all the makings

for some lunchmeat sandwiches. While he was crafting those, I took the opportunity to continue exploring his space. Past the kitchen, there was a decent sized bathroom sink, and a door that opened to a toilet and shower. Not huge, but also better than campground vault toilets. I kept going down the hallway and found the bedroom—queen size bed and a ton of closet space. *I could live in this.*

"Hey, does your department clean the vault toilets at the campground?" I asked out of the blue.

He burst out laughing. "What? Why are you asking about the vault toilets?"

"Oh, just something that crossed my mind when I was in there this morning. Who cleans them? What a horrible job—yuck!"

"Are they not clean?" he asked

"They are much better than most I've been in, which is why the question entered my mind."

"Yes, the Forest Service is responsible for maintaining campgrounds, so that does include the vault toilets. However, now that we have hosts, it is one of their duties to ensure everything stays as sanitary as possible. Occasionally, though, we have to bring out the honey bucket folks to suck it all out."

"Oh! That is *the worst job ever*!" I exclaimed.

"Thankfully, after more than twenty-five years with the department, toilet cleaning doesn't fall within my duties any longer. There are always newer and younger rangers coming in who get to get their hands wet doing the grunt work." He smiled. "Ready for lunch?" he asked laughing.

"It will be awhile before I'll be able to eat again. Let's get going though, we're losing daylight. C'mon Shadow—wanna go hike?" Oh boy did she! Her body started twisting and turning and she could barely contain her excitement and I couldn't open the door fast enough. Greg finished packing the lunch into his backpack and we headed out the door.

* * *

It was a gorgeous day out, temperatures still in the sixties and light cloud cover. Even so, I wore my hat and sunscreen to protect my skin from the sun. Today, I put on lightweight hiking pants and a long-sleeved shirt. It took us nearly an hour of driving just to get to the trailhead.

Shadow was off leash; the trail to Chevelon Canyon Lake was not busy at all and we enjoyed the quietness as we walked along the rocky trail. It's a rugged hike and not for the faint of heart ... just my cup of tea. After eight miles or so, we saw the sparkling reflection of the lake in the distance. Bracing for the steep downhill journey for the final mile to the water, we discovered that we were plenty hungry now and ready for a lunch break.

"I haven't been here in a long time. There are never too many people around because it isn't easy to get to ... so, it's a nice little respite," Greg said as he gazed around the area.

"It's gorgeous and peaceful. Hey, wait ... Shadow!" the flash of black racing past me and diving headlong into the lake made me quickly turn and almost lose my balance. This dog never passes down an opportunity to get wet.

"Looks like she's enjoying herself," Greg chuckled. "I brought a couple beers; would you like one?"

"Nah, just water for me." I took the water he handed over. "We have quite the hike out of here and I'm not sure I'd have the energy for it after a beer, I'd probably want to curl up and take a nap."

"Well, we should have thought of that and brought the sleeping bags. How cool would that be to sleep here lakeside overnight?"

"I'd *love* that!"

"So, different subject, but what did you make of that interaction with Charlie and the girl from the library?" Greg asked.

"Yeah, we never really discussed that did we? I was thinking they must know each other—their conversation appeared to be a little more intimate than just passing strangers or acquaintances. She also seemed afraid to me, at the library, and I can't figure that out."

"It was definitely odd. I don't know. Guess it's best to stay out of other people's business."

"I didn't want to say anything previously because it appeared you are good friends of Charlie and Julie's, but since we're talking about his behavior, do you ever get a strange feeling about him?" I asked.

"Well, first, it's not as though we are 'good friends'. I met them about a month or so ago when they showed up here for their forest service volunteer job. I stop by and talk with many different camp hosts—we try to keep lines of communication open. You know, I guess like cooperative forest service workers," he explained, then took a swig of his beer. "I may have gotten to know them a little bit more than others because they have that Tuesday night gathering."

"So, you don't notice anything 'off' about Charlie?"

"Oh, yeah, he's a strange little man for sure. But, what exactly are you asking?"

"There's something about him that creeps me out, but I

haven't one hundred percent identified what it is. He's nice enough. Seems helpful with this missing person search." I grabbed a few more chips and continued. "I think it's the way he stares at me. I'm probably just jumpy with all the investigation stuff going on. I mean, I really didn't think Isobel would actually be *missing* … so I think I'm surprised at that still and most likely sensitive? Like everyone is a suspect?"

Shadow came bounding up the slight incline from the lake, stopped right in front of us and shook off all the water on her coat.

"Shadow!! No!! *Ugh*…" I yelled out. I jumped up to get her away from the spread of food we had out.

Laughing, Greg finished off the last of his beer and then laid back to enjoy the midday sun. I ran Shadow around a bit to get her to finish shaking off water, away from our picnic lunch. It wasn't long before she was lying next to Greg in the sun and she was fully dry. *Hopefully she has energy left for the climb out. Aren't they cute soaking up the sun?*

"I could live out here," Greg said out of the blue.

"I know, it's incredible."

"I've often dreamed of retiring and setting out across the country in my RV. Someday it will happen. For now, though, I can't get enough of these hills and the beauty of the forest."

"That sounds amazing—the RV travel. I hope you get to do that."

"There are so many places I haven't been, I would love to see all the national parks. There are thousands of state parks throughout the country, too. I could probably spend the rest of my life on the road."

"In your RV, I could see that. It's definitely a home

on wheels. You have every comfort imaginable, that's for sure." I have always preferred the more rustic camping—in a tent, or even just a sleeping bag under the night sky.

I started gathering stuff up and getting it all back in our packs. Reluctantly, Greg and Shadow decided it was time to start the climb out and make the eight-mile hike back to the vehicle before we lost daylight.

* * *

"Is that Julie?" we had turned into our campsite and stepped out of the Tundra. Julie was running across the road, looking quite frantic.

"Have ... you ... seen him?" she tried to catch her breath and talk at the same time once she stopped in front of us.

We looked at each other and it seemed as though we both had the same thought. Clearly, she was asking about Charlie. *Do we tell her we saw him in town talking to that girl?* Thankfully Greg spoke up first as I stood there dumbfounded.

"Julie, what's wrong? Who are you talking about?"

"Charlie! He didn't come home last night!"

"Oh. Well ... we were in Heber at the library earlier. Libby saw one of the volunteers there and then when we left, we thought maybe he was speaking to her outside of the library over near the high school." Greg hesitantly explained. "He's helping out with the search, right?"

"There was no planned meeting at the library," Julie said. "I woulda heard 'bout it. Also doesn't 'splain where he been all night."

After an uncomfortable minute or two, and really

wanting to vanish, I instead chose to be a better person. I stepped forward and touched her arm in a comforting manner, and spoke in a soft voice, "Julie, I'm sure there's a good explanation, and he'll probably be home any minute."

"He's already missed supper time," she added, still upset.

"What would you like us to do?" Greg asked.

She started crying. "Oh, I really don't know …" she gasped between breaths. "He's been acting 'off' lately," she added with air quotes.

"How so?" *Maybe this has something to do about why I feel uncomfortable around him?*

"He seems gone away from camp more this week. We got work to be done around here, ya know! And, he's smellin' fresh and clean these days. I know, that seems weird to say 'bout my husband … but, why do you need aftershave in the mountains?"

"Oh. Well, maybe with the search and rescue and all the interactions with police, volunteers, forest service…" I pointed at Greg, "maybe he's trying to better present himself?"

She hung her head, twisting slightly from side to side. "Maybe. Hadn't thought about that. I s'pose he may be away helpin' with the search. Jus' don't know why he wouldn't call though."

"Well, why don't you pull up a chair here. I'll get you something to drink … what would you like: beer, water, wine, coffee…?"

"A beer sure would be nice!" she seemed to perk up a bit.

We all sat around having a drink and enjoying the fire Greg built. I tried to divert conversation to other subjects not having to do with Charlie, and it seemed to work for awhile. She settled down and actually enjoyed a laugh or two until Charlie's old beat-up Ford pulled into their place across the road.

Quickly standing up, knocking the camp chair over, hands on hips, she marched right over there with a scowl on her face. *Oh boy, hopefully Charlie has a good explanation.* We quietly went into the RV so we wouldn't hear the argument that ensued from there.

CHAPTER TEN

How late did they go on last night?" Greg asked, wondering if I got any sleep after Shadow and I ventured back to our tent the night before.

Pouring another cup of coffee and settling back into my chair, "I'm not entirely sure. I was so exhausted from the hike, I pretty much dropped right off. Shadow too. Slept like a baby."

"Good, I was worried you'd have another sleepless night."

"What's on your agenda today? You said you don't have to be back at work until Tuesday, right?" I asked Greg.

"I need to check with the SAR incident commander on this missing person's case. It's strange no one has called—either for an update or asking for our help. I sure hope they are still looking for Isobel."

"Yes, I was wondering about that too. And, I have to say that I'm more than curious about where Charlie was and what the story is there," I added.

"Seems like things quieted down with Jurgi and Juan … they haven't been around. I think I'll head into the office today for awhile and see what I can learn."

"Sounds like a plan. Shadow and I are going to take a rest day … it's Sunday after all, and that was quite a hike yesterday. I'm surprised at how sore I am today." I grimaced, making the point clearer.

After another cup of coffee each, Greg set off in Whitey. Shadow and I settled in for a morning of reading and being quiet. Just what the doctor ordered. Of course, as soon as I was really getting into the story, my phone started ringing.

"Hi JJ!"

"Libby, how are things up north?"

"Shadow and I are loving the cooler weather and we've got a lot of good hiking in since we've been here. However, I'm still concerned about Isobel and there doesn't seem to be much progress in the search. Of course, Greg is learning more about that today … maybe I'm wrong?"

"Greg?" JJ inquired.

"Oh, uh … the forest service ranger friend."

"Oh, yeah, the hunky guy with the blue eyes…" JJ teased, but quickly got back on the reason for his call. "Listen, Libby … I have some more information I thought you'd be interested in."

"Yes, go on…"

"You had texted me about the ranch you discovered and its ownership."

I completely forgot about texting him the question before I was distracted at the library that day with the volunteer … and then Charlie. "Oh, yes. What did you learn?"

"Well, the ranch has been owned for decades by the Crenshaw family … a Daniel Crenshaw purchased the land back in the thirties. He's long since passed, but I imagine it's been passed down in the family since there's no record of it being resold since that time."

My heart started pounding. Crenshaw. *Maggie Crenshaw? Is she a descendant?*

Without divulging my surprise at his news, I thanked JJ for his report and asked about Alexis and Joshua before hanging up. *I need to get home.*

No sooner than I had hung up with JJ, Julie was walking up. "Howdy, neighbor," she called out.

"Hi there. So, what happened to Charlie? Where was he?" I couldn't hold back the questions; I was so curious.

"I guess he was working the case, and his phone died," she said confidently, as though she bought his story.

"Ok. I'm relieved he was okay and nothing was wrong then." I didn't believe that story. And, why were they going on and on, arguing late into the night?

"Yep, he was real sweet on me once all the yellin' stopped. He's quite the lover …"

I quickly interjected, not wanting to hear any details of their love life, "Are there any new details about the search for Isobel? Seems like they must have been onto something if it took all night?"

A curious look crossed her face. "I didn't ask," she said quietly.

"Oh, ok. Well, Greg will learn more today at the office."

"Anyway, I wanted to stop by and say thanks for the beer last night and distractin' me for a bit. I 'preciate it," she said, almost uncomfortably.

"Absolutely, anytime."

It was clear that was all she wanted when she turned to head back to her camp. Not long after that, I heard Charlie's side-by-side start up. *He must be heading out for his rounds.*

I tried to get back to reading and relaxing but all I could think of was the information that JJ had given me. I needed to talk to Maggie more, but not over the phone. As I was contemplating the questions I had for her, Charlie drove into my camp, parked his cart, and marched over to me as though he meant business.

"Stay out of my marriage!" he spat right into my face.

"Hey, whoa! Charlie, back off …" I moved back several steps. "You know there's a virus going around, don't talk so close to my face!" With space between us now, "What is the problem here?"

He moved to step closer, and I moved back again. Pointing his finger at me, he started yelling again, "You are meddlin' and I don't appreciate it. Now I'm in trouble with the missus."

"C'mon Charlie. Julie came to us worried about where you've been! How is that meddling?" I argued.

"You tol' her 'bout a girl…"

"We told her that you may be working the case because we last saw you talking to one of the volunteers near the library in town."

"You're messing in business that's not yours!" he yelled.

"Wait just a minute. It's *my* friend that is missing—that *is* my business. Your wife asked me a question—I answered it. And, you were working on the search for Isobel—at least that's what you told Julie, right? So, what exactly have

I got wrong here? And, why the hell did you run off from that school near the library?"

"I don't know what you're talking about? I wasn't near any school," he said.

"Charlie," I spoke quietly, trying to cool down the temperature of the conversation, "you looked right at us and then you and the girl ran off in separate directions. We were only coming over to ask about the search for Isobel. Why run?"

"Never saw you."

Something was definitely fishy, but it was clear this was going nowhere. At least he had calmed down slightly, though there was a moment there I was sure he would strike out at me.

"Ok. Well, it's time for you to go … and don't worry, I'll stay out of your business." Thankfully, he did turn and leave.

* * *

With the information that JJ had given me about the ranch property earlier, I decided to pack up my belongings and head back to the city. I was nearly home when my phone rang.

"Why didn't you wait for me?" Greg immediately asked when I picked up the call.

"I know. I feel horrible running off so fast. I tried calling you, but knew you'd be busy for awhile so I didn't want to pester. Did you get my note?"

"Left on the RV door, yep … got it. I was stunned that you're all packed up and gone. I thought we had a couple more days before you were going to leave?" he said almost with a whine in his tone, but yet irritated at the same time.

"Sorry, Greg. A couple things happened since you left for the ranger station and I just needed to get back home. I'll give you a call later when I know more." I hated to cut it short, but at the same time, I wasn't in any mood to talk. I'd been stewing for the past hour over that altercation with Charlie and I truly didn't want to take it out on any innocent bystanders.

My first inclination was to get in touch with Maggie, but then what exactly was it that I wanted to know from her? She wasn't being forthright with me, but I didn't exactly have anything concrete that proved it. *Who was this boyfriend of hers? Where was this boyfriend of hers?*

As soon as I had set my armload of camping gear down on my sofa, I took Shadow outside in the backyard. On the way back into the house, and passing by the kitchen counter covered in mail I hadn't opened yet, I noticed my answering machine blinking. Yes, I still have that archaic device … just haven't had the nerve to give up my landline yet even though I almost exclusively use my cell phone now.

Hitting the play button, I saw I missed several calls … apparently, Alexis forwarded some spa calls my way. The first two were confirming already scheduled appointments for a few days from now. The last one was Maggie wanting to schedule a session for tomorrow. *Well, look at that! There's my reason for calling her.*

"Hi Maggie, it's Libby. Just got your message. You want to schedule a session for tomorrow?" I said cheerfully.

"Libby," she barely whispered, almost as though she was out of breath.

"Maggie? Are you ok?" I asked.

"Li—Libby." Again, it was a faint whisper of a voice. So unlike Maggie.

"Maggie, what's wrong? Do you need me to come over?"

The line went dead.

Holy crap. What on earth is going on with her?

* * *

Leaving Shadow in her crate at home, I pulled up in front of Maggie's home in central Mesa. I saw her SUV and several of the broken-down vehicles, but no Bronco. *Ok, good. Not sure I want to deal with Mr. Grumpus today.*

I knocked on the door first. No answer.

After knocking a second time, I decided to try the door handle and discovered it was unlocked. Opening the door slowly, I called out, "Maggie?"

"Maggie!" I yelled out again, and proceeded to walk down the hall, looking into the kitchen to the left. When I didn't see her there, I entered the room at the end of the hall, my eyes scanning the living room … it was dark, but I could see the leather recliner and a medium-sized blue loveseat facing an older TV. She wasn't in the room so I yelled out her name again.

Following another hallway to the right of the living room, I picked up my pace and started opening closed doors, frantically calling out, "Maggie! Where are you?" At the end of the hallway, the third door that I opened, I saw her asleep in her bed. *Please, please, just be asleep!*

I reached into my pocket for my mask, put it on, and walked over to her side and reached out to lightly touch her arm. Gently, I said her name and gave her a nudge.

Thank God—she's warm. I listened for her breathing. She was breathing, so I shook her a little harder, "Maggie, wake up!" I said louder.

"Lib…" she started to slur and her eyes fluttered open slightly.

"Maggie! What on earth is going on? Did you take something?" *Should I be calling 911?*

"Libby," she whispered. "I tire—d."

"I see that. Are you not feeling well? Did you take some medicine?"

"No. Jus' tire …"

"What did you take? I'm getting worried; this is not normal."

"John…" her eyes rolled up in her head and she was gone.

"MAGGIE! What about John?" I shook her, but she was out again. I checked her pulse and it was faint. Her breathing was becoming labored too. *Time to call paramedics.*

As I was waiting for the paramedics to arrive, I took it upon myself to search the bathroom vanity. My eyes were transfixed the moment I opened the mirrored medicine cabinet. *What? How can someone have sooo many prescriptions? I didn't remember her listing all these on her health questionnaire at the spa.* I heard the ambulance pull up, so I ran for the door.

"I found her in here … hurry!" I led them through the house.

There were four EMTs; three of them immediately went to Maggie and started assessing her vitals. The fourth handsome fire fighter pulled me out of the room, down the hall, and into the living room. I relayed all the details as I knew them … which wasn't much, other than I was worried about how she sounded on the phone and then I rushed over and found her drugged up.

"You will want to see her medicine cabinet. It's full of prescriptions, but I have no idea what she may have taken today."

"Has she been distraught lately? Any sign of depression?" he asked me.

"Oh, no!" *Did she try to kill herself?* "That's something else. Her daughter went missing a week or so ago. So, yes, depression … I'm sure … I'm sure … she is depressed." I said hanging my head low. *How had I missed this? I should have stayed around here more and let the police do their job up north! Of course, she's distraught!*

The other paramedics were already transporting her out to the ambulance while I finished telling everything that I knew. I found a bag in the kitchen so they could gather up all the pill bottles—I guess for evidence?

I looked and looked around the house for a phone number for John. There was no cell phone anywhere I could see—*doesn't Maggie have a cell phone? I have no idea what John's last name is! How do I reach him?* I watched helplessly as she was taken away to the hospital and I had no idea who to call.

Please be okay Maggie.

CHAPTER ELEVEN

"Lex ... hi!" I mustered up some positivity in my voice. After a sleepless night, it was the last thing I was feeling at the moment. "Yes, yes ... I'm back in town now."

"Oh, I'm so happy to hear that! I sent a few messages your way and then remembered it could be a few more days until you got them. Stupid me!" she said so cheerfully. It was so good to hear her voice after all I had been through in the last twenty-four hours.

"Listen, Lex ... I have bad news. My client, Maggie ... she's in the hospital. I found her barely conscious late yesterday and called to have her taken to emergency."

Alexis inhaled sharply, "Oh no! Please tell me she's going to be okay?"

"I sure hope so. I'm calling over there next to see if I can get any status on her condition. They won't allow visitors due to the virus. Listen—I want to catch up with you soon, but for now, can I talk to JJ? He was looking into something for me."

"Sure, no problem. And yes, as soon as you're available, let's get together for tea or lunch. I miss my best friend!" she pleaded.

I waited as I heard her hunt down her husband. I could hear Joshua laughing and playing in the background. *I can't wait to get together with the whole family again—really miss them.*

"Hey Libs, what's up?" JJ asked.

"Oh, JJ … I'm feeling completely overwhelmed by this missing girl case … the Crenshaws." Suddenly, I couldn't remember how much I'd told him about the whole case, but he seemed to step right in with me.

"Have they found her yet?" he asked.

"No. And no sightings or leads. It's getting really frustrating."

"And the information about the ranch property didn't help?"

"Well, that's just it. I feel like it definitely has something to do with it, but I don't know how. And now Maggie Crenshaw is in the ICU—possible drug overdose."

"Did you say overdose?"

"Yes, why?"

"Remember I told you there were numerous visits from CPS over the years? Well, upon further investigation with a buddy of mine at Child Protective Services, Maggie seemed to take Isobel to various specialists *all the time.*"

"Yes, but I know she had asthma and diabetes so I'm sure that equated to numerous visits over the years?" I wasn't sure where he was going with this when it struck me like lightning. "OH, wait! I helped the paramedics gather the prescription bottles we found at the scene, and I couldn't help but notice many had Isobel's name on them!"

"What type of medications?" he asked.

"I really don't know. We were in such a hurry that I didn't pay much attention. In fact, I didn't immediately notice it … only once they were pulling away did I remember that not all the bottles had Maggie's name on them. I'm sure the doctors noticed this when they went through that bag." *Did any of them have Maggie's name on them?*

"Ok. So, what does that tell us?" he continued questioning.

"That Isobel is a sickly kid?" I reckoned, and then I had an ah-ha moment. "And how would someone that sick go off *hiking with her boyfriend?*"

"You know, Libby, I'm going to give my buddy up north another call. I want to see if I can question the boyfriend … with his attorney present, of course."

"What are you thinking, JJ?"

"I want to learn more about the relationship between Maggie and Isobel from *his* perspective."

* * *

I needed some fresh air so Shadow and I headed out for a run before it got too hot out. Turning right at the end of my street, we ran toward our favorite spot out in the open desert. There was a trail we could follow and we rarely ever came across others so I let Shadow off leash and we proceeded at a brisk run for nearly four miles.

"Here sweetie," I had taken a large swig of water from my bottle and then poured some into the cup of my other hand and offered it to Shadow. She lapped it right up. "Ok, ready … let's go home!"

Prior to the run, my head was spinning and felt enormously full of all the input I'd received over the past week. Now as we were approaching the housing development again, I realized how necessary this exercise was—to prevent me from having a complete meltdown. We stopped and I clipped Shadow's leash back on and we did our cool down as we walked through the neighborhood for about ten minutes before we made it back home.

The phone was ringing as I opened the door. I ran for it and breathlessly answered, "Hello, this is Libby…"

"Libby Madsen?"

"This is she!" I started feeling that runner's high and had so much more energy.

"Hello, this is Carolyn from Banner Desert Medical. We had in our notes that you were with Margaret Crenshaw when she collapsed yesterday. Do you have time for a few questions?"

"Yes, I was with her. She didn't really collapse per se, she was in bed when I arrived at her house. How is she doing? Is she awake yet?"

"Ms. Crenshaw is in a medically induced coma. She was critical when she arrived here—later when she was coming to, she … well, she had a series of seizures. We've made her a little more comfortable and when her vitals are more stable again, we'll start lowering the meds."

"Oh my …" And, there went my newfound energy.

"Ms. Madsen, can you tell us if there is anyone that lives in the Crenshaw residence other than Margaret?"

"She has a boyfriend. I'm not entirely sure, but I don't think he's been around all week."

"Ok. Well, someone has been administering meds to

her and we need to speak to that person. Were you giving her medication?"

"Uh, no. Why? Wh- what makes you think someone was drugging her?"

"We're waiting for some more labs to come back but, from what we can figure out so far, she's been slowly fed some very powerful drugs. The way we know it wasn't self-administered is because at the levels that are in her bloodstream, she would barely be able to move."

I was stunned. "Ok. Well, I know that her boyfriend's name is John. Unfortunately, that's all I know. I don't know his last name. Oh, and her daughter is missing…"

"You've been helpful Ms. Madsen, thank you. We're going to have to report this to the police. We believe there is something nefarious going on and we have to protect our patient."

"Will I be able to visit Maggie soon?"

"Unfortunately, with the virus going around, no visitors are allowed. Not even next of kin." She said her goodbyes and hung up.

I sat down and gulped the rest of my water.

How did I get mixed up in all this? Where is Isobel? She'd be so worried about her mother! I have to call Greg—

I finished washing up, got out of the shower, and put on fresh clean shorts and a t-shirt before I tried to reach Greg. Back in the kitchen, I fixed myself a high fiber, protein smoothie and then waited for Greg to answer his phone.

"Hey, hey there … I was starting to wonder about you!" He had answered so cheerfully.

"Hi! It's so good to hear a friendly voice. You won't believe the morning I've had. No, make that … the last twenty-four hours actually."

"Oh yeah, you never told me what occurred to drive you away, literally, yesterday. Is everything ok, Libby?" He sounded worried.

I got him all caught up on the altercation with Charlie, JJ's information about Maggie and the CPS visits throughout Isobel's childhood, the ranch land that belongs to the Crenshaw family, and then finally Maggie's hospitalization.

"Holy crap, you've been dealing with a ton of sh…" he stopped himself, "stuff, Libby."

"Yeah, and I'm sitting here now wondering exactly how I've got myself caught up in all this? It's really crazy. And from what the nurse was saying on the phone earlier, they suspect that Maggie was being drugged. Why? To keep her quiet? Does this have to do with Isobel's disappearance?"

"It's hard not to believe they're related, huh?"

"Greg, I really need to find Isobel. Her mother is in the hospital now!"

"I wish I had good news for you on that front. Unfortunately, the search hasn't turned up anything new."

"Don't you find it extremely odd that the ranch is owned by the Crenshaws, but Maggie has never mentioned to me anything about it? In fact, when I told her I was going up to the Rim and would help look for Isobel, she acted as though she'd never been there before."

"That is interesting. Maybe it was distant relatives and she *hasn't* ever been up there?"

"Maybe Isobel knows of the place and wanted to find it … maybe got lost?"

"Still doesn't explain why she was supposed to be with Rod and then wasn't," I added.

"Wait. Libby. Remember you thought you saw movement in that house through the window?"

Chills ran up my spine. I had totally forgotten about that. "Yes. Go on…"

"Do you suppose she could be … or someone could be … hiding her there?"

"Why wouldn't they have answered the door when we banged on it?" I asked.

"Because they're *hiding*. Or, someone is hiding her … she *can't* get to the door."

I literally felt sick at his last words. Could we have possibly been that close to her? *Oh God!*

Greg broke into my thoughts, "I'm heading over there now. I'll try to get one of the police officers to go too, but I'm not sure … without a warrant and all. Regardless, I'm going to go see what I can learn."

"Please be careful, Greg."

I had just hung up with him, when my phone immediately start ringing again.

"Well, hello there … it's been awhile," I greeted Sage. She has been a client since before we started our spa, when we only offered mobile service. "How are you?"

"Oh, Libby … I'm so happy you answered! I'm doing ok, but I could really use some work done on my lower back. It's been bothering me again and I was hoping I could get in with you sooner than later."

"Well, you're in luck. I could potentially see you this afternoon, but I have to ask… when were you last tested for the virus? With things pretty much closed down, have you been isolating? We've had to close the doors to the spa for several weeks, and we have to follow fairly strict protocols for mobile service these days."

"Please don't worry, I haven't gone anywhere since this virus started ... just been isolated here at home for weeks. I could go get a test, but I seriously haven't been around anyone else. What about you?"

Ah, good question. "I'm getting tested twice a week right now in order to continue seeing clients. I would be willing to do a rapid test this morning; I have been around several others since my last test. So, let's do that ... based on that outcome, I could plan on being to your house around 2 p.m.?"

"That would be fantastic! I'll wait to hear from you. You still know where to find me?" Sage asked.

"Of course. Ok, see you this afternoon."

* * *

Before running to the drugstore for the test, I remembered that JJ was already up in Show Low talking to Rod where he was being detained. *I wonder if he could go out to the ranch with Greg?*

"Hi JJ, please call me when you get the message. They've kept Maggie in an induced coma, but the call from the hospital this morning was strange. I think they suspect foul play here. Anyway, call me!" Disappointed, I hung up my phone. I was really hoping that I could quickly coordinate Greg and JJ to meet up and help each other on this case. Oh well.

I took Shadow out one last time before I headed out the door. I was feeling scattered and confused by all that I'd learned this morning. Focusing on a client would be just the thing to calm me down.

After receiving my negative test, I stopped by the spa

to grab clean sheets. Opening the door, I could tell Alexis
was here even though I hadn't seen her vehicle out front.

"Alexis!" I called as I entered so I wouldn't scare her.

"Back here!" I followed the sound of her voice by
walking through the first set of frosted glass doors, through
the serenity room, another set of glass doors which were
propped open, and then, through the open door, I saw her
sitting at her desk.

"Hey, what are you doing here today?" I asked her.

"I could ask you the same question," she said as she
stood, came around her desk, and embraced me. "I'm just
catching up on laundry and paperwork."

"It feels like we haven't seen each other in ages and
really it's only been about a week," I said with a bit of a
pout. "I miss my bestie! Hey, why don't we get lunch …
tomorrow?"

"Yes, let's! We'll have to do it at your house or mine …
restaurants are still closed for indoor dining."

"True. Or, how about we run through Senor Taco
drive-thru and head over to the park. They have good shade
and we could do a little picnic in the fresh air instead?" I
suggested.

"Sounds like a great plan! I believe JJ plans on being
home tonight so he should be able to stay with Joshua so
we can have a girls-only lunch."

"Cool! Well, I've gotta grab a set of clean sheets and
I'm headed over to Sage's home—she's okay with a regular
90-minute session. We'll get back to her preferred Ashiatsu
sessions when we re-open the spa for clients."

"Speaking of which, when I was talking to a friend
of mine at City Hall, she thinks the restrictions should be
lifted within a couple weeks. I was afraid it may go longer,

but cases are declining and the governor is considering lifting his executive order. That would be great, huh?"

"Indeed! Ok, I'm out of here!" I gave my friend a hug, got what I needed for the therapy session, and headed out.

* * *

I think I'm having mixed feelings over things opening back up. I sort of like doing the mobile sessions and getting out and about more often. It sure has afforded me more time in the mountains recently so I can't complain about that. However, we can't stay in business if we aren't filling the appointment slots more regularly—and I *love* our beautiful space—so I do recognize the importance of getting it reopened.

Still lost in my thoughts as I pulled up to Sage's ranch style home on the outskirts of town, I pulled down the long drive and then turned Trina around and backed up toward the front door of the home so I could unload. Sage waved from the front patio as I got out of my vehicle and put on my mask.

It was so beautiful where she lived, with a view of the Superstition Mountains and decent acreage so houses weren't right next to one another as they are in most housing developments. Her bougainvillea in several spots along the front of her house were in full bloom—beautiful reds and corals accented the tan adobe house with dark trim. She has a small studio to the right of the main house just off the front patio. She's an artist and spends much of her time in the studio.

"Good afternoon!" she said as I walked up. "Gorgeous day, isn't it?"

"You know, it's always stunning out here. Yours is my favorite home to come to!" I followed her into the casita and got right to work, quickly getting my massage table set up with sheets in place and ready to go.

Relaxing spa music was already playing in the room and she had started one of her essential oil diffusers with a lavender spearmint blend. "Wow, you've set up a perfect room for us to do this!" I commented. "I'll step out while you undress to your comfort level. Let's start you face down."

Sage was a beautiful soul—blonde long flowing hair, crystal blue eyes. She was maybe five foot five and slightly heavy for her frame. In her mid-fifties now, she had retired from nursing a couple years ago to pursue her art and spirituality. Her husband passed just before she decided to retire and I think that actually helped her to make the decision. They had purchased the home outside of the city with the hopes of retiring one day, but nothing was concrete until after she had mourned her loss. That was about the point in time when she became a client of mine. She preferred more quiet sessions and didn't talk a whole lot. However, on occasion, she would open up and I would learn these little tidbits from her.

Kneading deep along her superior muscles on her back, and near the scapula, I became entranced with the music, at the same time working through knots and helping to elongate the muscle segments. My mind wandered and I wondered where Greg was at this moment. JJ hadn't called before I walked into my appointment so I doubted getting those two together would be a possibility at this point.

"Libby, have you seen the news of that young girl that's gone missing?" Sage broke into my thoughts.

"Isobel?" I asked, surprised that she'd know anything about it.

"Yes, on the evening news they mentioned that there are search and rescue looking for her up north. I couldn't help but think I've seen her before when they showed her smiling face on TV."

"Do you know her?"

"Laying here with my eyes closed, I just remembered that I think she came into the same pediatric hospital that I was at for a number of years."

"Really? Talk about a small world," I marveled.

"If this truly is the same girl, and if my memory is serving me well at all—you know, it is failing me more and more—I seem to remember she and her mother coming in fairly frequently."

"Do you know her mother?"

"Um, let me see … her name … it wasn't something all that common…" Sage got quiet, searching the silence for the answer. "Margaret, maybe?"

"Ok, this really is strange, Sage. Margaret is a client of mine. Two weeks ago, she was telling me that her daughter went camping and she was a little concerned since she had expected her back the night before. I go hiking and camping in the same area she was supposed to be going, so I told Maggie I'd take a look around." I covered Sage's back, moved to her legs, and adjusted the privacy sheet to expose her left leg. "I never found her, but they found the boyfriend and also some personal effects of hers so it's now a search and rescue operation."

"Oh, wow. I had no idea you'd be involved. I'm so sorry for her mother."

"Well, it seems to be getting stranger by the day. Now

Maggie is in the hospital. I went over to visit with her after my last venture to the Rim and found her unconscious. To me, it appeared it was an overdose ... and, with her daughter missing, who could blame her?"

Sage sighed. "I cannot even imagine. And, from what I remember about her, she was super obsessed with her daughter. I mean like complete hypervigilant mom. I remember making remarks to my colleagues that she almost *enjoyed* being at the hospital. I know that sounds strange, but she would bring Isobel in for *every little thing.*"

"What was wrong with Isobel that she was in the hospital so much?" I inquired, hoping to learn more than I already had.

"As I recall, it started with things like colds and we would explain that doesn't warrant being hospitalized. Later, it seemed to be a myriad of stuff: stomach aches, appendicitis, possible meningitis, weakness and extreme fatigue. There always seemed to be something, but we rarely actually found out what was wrong. Fairly vague symptoms, but her mom was adamant that we needed to check for specific diseases. Talk about paranoid with her first child!"

"Hey, was there ever a boyfriend, or perhaps Isobel's dad, that came with her to the hospital?"

"Never. Always only mother and daughter." Sage rolled over to her back when directed, and I continued working on the front side of her legs and feet. "I sure hope they find her."

"Me too."

We both fell back into our own thoughts as I proceeded to massage her arms, then shoulders, neck, and head. Every time I worked on Sage, I absorbed peaceful feelings from her. A warmth and kindness that exuded without words ever being spoken. She calmed me which was ironic since I was the one who was massaging *her*.

Feeling so refreshed after my appointment with Sage, I decided I was going to make a nice light early dinner, take a bubble bath, and just relax for the evening. There were plenty of vegetables in the refrigerator, and I pulled out the InstaPot where I loaded it up with onion, garlic, broccoli, carrots, potatoes, basmati rice and my favorite tikka masala sauce from a bottle. *A vegetable curry sounds perfect! Maybe a glass of Pinot to go with that? Ahhhh…*

The phone rang. *Why didn't I turn off my ringer?* Looking at the display, I saw it was Greg.

"Hi Greg, anything new where you are?"

"Well, I think I found Isobel," he stated as a matter-of-fact.

CHAPTER TWELVE

You did?!" I nearly shouted; I was so surprised.

"Well, I can't be one hundred percent sure. I decided not to drive up to the ranch house, but instead, I hiked in from that back road ... you know, the one we found last week?"

"Yep ... go on..."

"Through my binoculars, I watched the whole property for a couple hours. No Bronco—no John. As I was about to give up and call it a day, there was movement near the barn. Out came a young woman ... petite, blonde. She was carrying something from the barn and then entered the house from that side door we found, closest to the barn-side."

"Then what happened?" I asked.

"That's just it. Nothing. I figured it would be the

exact same situation as you and I ran into. If I went to the door, she'd ignore it. I don't have a warrant; I can't enter the premises. So, I've called the State Police with the information that I do have ... they'll obtain a warrant and identify the person I saw."

"Oh my goodness! I really hope it is her!" I couldn't contain my excitement. "Seems peculiar ... is she hiding out there? Doesn't seem to be held captive if she's walking about the property and not running to try to get away, right?"

"Yes, that's exactly what I thought and why I didn't want to approach and possibly drive her into hiding. This whole thing keeps getting stranger."

"Oh, I meant to tell you ... I tried calling you earlier, but didn't reach you ... a friend of mine, JJ—who also happens to be a cop down here in Mesa—headed up that direction hoping to speak to Rod."

"Really? What would he speak to him about?" Greg asked.

"He's been helping me out with a few things. The first thing he discovered is that CPS has been called out to the Crenshaw home numerous times during Isobel's childhood. I always took Maggie for being a nice, caring mother so that shocked me. But, there's more ... he said that in those reports are details of *many* hospital visits."

"Whoa, child abuse? Is that what you're thinking?"

"Well, yeah. What I can't figure out is who the abuser is; Maggie, the father of Isobel, or a random boyfriend? I mean, look at John ... he scares the hell out of me—what was he doing to Isobel? But, even more confusing, Isobel is in her early twenties—if abused, *why* would she still live her in mother's home?"

"Holy crap, Libby. And yes, good question … I'd move out—or run away—at the very first opportunity!"

"And then, just today … one of my clients happens to ask if I'd seen anything on the news about that missing girl. Yes, she meant Isobel! Well, it turns out that she was a pediatric nurse years back and she remembers Isobel and her mother coming into her unit *many times*. She didn't say as much, but I suspect she may have been the one who called CPS on this family." I took another swig of my white wine, released the steam on the InstaPot, and went to grab a bowl from the cabinet.

"This is definitely information the State Police should have," Greg added. "Hey, you said your friend JJ was here to talk to Rod. He'll have to coordinate with the State Police to get that access."

"Yes, He said he knew a local sheriff guy…"

"Maybe I could try to meet up with him … I know several top guys in Show Low. That could help get him in sooner. Plus, I have Rod's lawyer's contact information. No one will get in to talk to him without his lawyer present."

"Greg, that's a fantastic idea!" I gave him JJ's number.

"Sounds like you are fixing dinner, I should probably let you go. I'll get right on with the police and JJ; when I know more, I'll give you a ring."

"Ok, keep me informed. I'm going to check in on Maggie in the morning—I'm really hoping she'll come out of this and, more than anything else, I hope we have this CPS business all wrong and she and Isobel can happily reunite." We said our goodbyes and I settled back in with my nice warm curry and another glass of wine.

* * *

Despite a long hot bath, two glasses of wine, and a belly full of comforting food, I still had a restless night of sleep. I must have had one long continuous dream. I was running through the forest one moment, then listening through a stethoscope on some random person's chest the next. There were bunnies everywhere, and then sheep ... as though the bunnies grew up super-fast into these large sheep. I woke with a start when one of the sheep handed me a little booklet. *Jeez, Libby! No more wine before bed!*

It was still pre-dawn, but I roused Shadow and we went outside for fresh air. I brewed some coffee and after one cup, I decided we needed exercise. With Shadow's bra on and leash clasped, we headed out the front door just as the sun was barely beginning to light the morning sky. There were some random low-lying clouds that were turning a pinkish hue as the horizon began its fire orange glow. Stunning!

As we ran through the neighborhood and then out into our familiar desert trails, I couldn't help but go back to the dreams I'd had. Were they telling me something? I couldn't put my finger on it, but I felt pulled to go back to Maggie's house. I shivered, *Ugh, that place is a hell hole! Why, Libby ... why are you torturing yourself like this?*

Shadow ran off after a bunny. "Shadow!!" I yelled. She stopped. Then she turned and started after the bunny again. "SHADOW!!" She must have understood that mom means business that time because she abruptly turned and ran back in my direction. "You get the leash again, little girl ... thank you for coming back, but you can't run off like that." I spoke sweetly to her as I clipped on her leash so she knew she did a good thing by coming back to me.

Yep, my mind was made up ... after lunch with Alexis,

I'd go back to Maggie's. I did have a key now since I locked up her house after the EMTs hauled her off to the hospital. *Nope, not breaking and entering … I'm perfectly justified going into my friend's house and … and, getting some of her clothing for when she's released! Yeah, that's why I need to go inside!* Pleased with myself, we headed home.

* * *

"I'd like two shredded beef tacos, two shredded chicken tacos, a cheese quesadilla, and two medium iced teas. Mild sauce, please." I spoke extra loudly into the intercom device at the drive-thru window. I pulled forward to the window, paid, and gathered the food bag and drinks, securing them in the holders in my car.

As I pulled into the parking lot, I could see that Alexis and Joshua were already there sitting on a couple seats under one of the park-provided pavilions. The park was nearly deserted, which was nice … we almost had the whole place to ourselves. As I walked up, Joshua came running toward me and gave my leg a big hug.

"Whoa there, big boy, I've got my hands full. Can you carry this bag over to your mom?" He snatched it and ran off.

"I guess JJ didn't make it back from the hills last night?" I asked Alexis, as she was coming in for the big hug that I always get from my dear friend.

"I talked to him before bedtime and he said that he's bunking at Greg's. I didn't even know they knew each other?" she said almost suspiciously.

"Oh good, they made contact! I gave Greg his number … there have been some developments in our case."

Look at me, 'our case' … as though I'm some private investigator or something!

"Yeah, he was telling me that he talked to that girl's boyfriend. I guess the police were trying to secure a search warrant for some place?" She unwrapped her first taco and took a big bite, then swallowed it down with iced tea. "Anyway, I haven't heard him so excited in a while. Uh, just to be clear, I don't mean excited as though any of what's going on is *fun*. I know the lawman inside him is excited to help with this. So, that's where he is … helping."

I was nearly done with my chicken taco, holding up my finger in a 'wait a second' gesture while I got done chewing. "Did he tell you what he learned from Rod? Er, the boyfriend…" I asked.

"So, yeah … this seems crazy to me. Did you know that Isobel was chomping at the bit to get away from her mom?"

My eyes widened in surprise, "I always thought the two were super close. According to Maggie, mind you."

"Hmmm, apparently the picture that Rod painted was exactly the opposite. He told JJ that they met a couple years ago online. Chatted a lot—both on the phone and online, but he had not actually met her in person."

"Ok, that I didn't know. In fact, I didn't even know there was a boyfriend until just days ago. And according to Maggie's reaction, I'm fairly sure she knew nothing of the sort either." I tore off a big chunk out of the quesadilla and bit down into it. My eyes rolled back in my head with ecstasy. "You have to try this! Wow, so yummy."

She did and we both stopped speaking momentarily while we devoured the scrumptious warm gooey melted cheese wrapped up in a huge homemade flour tortilla. Delicious.

"I guess he felt bad for her because her mother was super controlling and she really never got to leave the house much on her own. Apparently, she was a sickly kid and mom doted over her. Eventually that wore thin as she became a teenager. I get it. I mean, could you imagine still living at home in your early twenties?" Alexis stopped to see my reaction.

"This is … well, honestly, I'm stunned. This is not the picture I had in my head of Maggie and her daughter at all."

"Mom, can I go to the playground? It's just right there." Joshua pointed to a sandy area with swings, monkey bars, and a climbing structure with bright yellow tubes for slides.

"Sure, go run around and have fun, sweetie!"

I sat back and took a deep breath. "Did Rod divulge anything else?"

"I think the gist was that he really fell for this girl online, she came up with a plan to go camping and told him where to go and she'd meet him. Then she never showed up and eventually, he learned she was officially missing. JJ said he legitimately seems distraught over the whole thing."

"It's too bad he ran from the cops. He'd probably be home by now if he hadn't," I said.

"That's basically what JJ's opinion was too."

"Oh! But, there is more, and JJ may not have known this yet when he talked to you last night. The reason that Greg went to the police, and why they are trying to get the search warrant, is because Greg thinks he may have seen Isobel!" I exclaimed.

"What? That's great! That means this whole mess could be over?" she asked.

"I think so. I haven't heard anything this morning yet, but I sure hope they call soon."

We then turned the conversation more to business and commiserating about our mobile appointments. Both of us agreed that we are really ready to get the spa doors open again. We spent a good hour dreaming of everything our business could be ... brainstorming ideas for specials, gaining new clients, and even our newest addition for the physical therapy wing.

"If Arizona PT accepts our lease agreement, we can get that entire thousand-foot space rented, completely renovated, and then their monthly rent will pay our entire spa mortgage. Crossing fingers they don't delay too long, or back out altogether," Alexis said, holding up her crossed fingers.

Dreaming, my arms swept out in front me as though I were in the room, "I can see it now ... a hydrotherapy circuit complete with hot tubs, a swim spa, a cold waterfall, and then the sauna."

"That's what's in the contract. It's exciting, isn't it?"

"It really will enhance our offerings at the spa. What other massage therapy place in town has entire sports or physical therapy type services *in the same location*?" I asked, as I was crumpling up our wrappers.

"Mom! C'mere!!" Joshua was yelling from the slide.

Alexis headed off toward her son and I threw all our trash away and joined them.

"Catch me!" the sweet boy yelled as he flung himself down the slide. Alexis caught him and lifted him high in the air and twirled around before setting him back to earth.

I jumped on a swing and started the movement back and forth. Legs straight out, leaning far backward ... then, legs bent back and torso forward. Over and over and I was swinging high. "I forget how much fun this is! Why don't we swing as adults?" I yelled over to Alexis.

"Ummm, 'swinging for adults' generally takes on a whole different connotation, Libby," she laughed and then she and Joshua joined me on the swings.

"Oh! You know I didn't mean that!"

We played around for another half an hour or so and then begrudgingly, we decided we each needed to get back to our day. I still wanted to snoop around Maggie's house (I mean, pick up some clothes for her), and Alexis had a massage appointment at two.

"Well, we sure need to do this more often. I'm almost happy the restaurants are closed, otherwise, we would have sat there inside. We would have missed out on fresh air and *playing*." Alexis had that mischievous look in her eye as she looked around the park.

"Yeah, Mom, we have to do this more often!" Joshua ran around in circles with his arms in the air, which led all of us to start doing the same.

Laughing and falling onto the grass, "I've never had more fun … UGH…" Joshua leaped right onto to me. I hefted him straight up above me and shook him around a bit teasingly.

"Ok, time to go, Joshua!" Alexis started to walk toward our vehicles. We got up off the grass and followed.

"If you hear from JJ, please ask him or Greg to give me a call. I really want to find out what is going on up there."

"Will do! See you tomorrow?" she asked.

"Yep, I'll stop in sometime around ten. I've got an 11:30 appointment with Mr. Lindler."

* * *

The house wasn't any less awful this afternoon. *Is it all the junk laying around, or why do I feel creeped out here?* I didn't see any new vehicles here; there was no Bronco—thank God. Even so, I parked a block over and out of sight, walking up to their property and observing the neighborhood as I did. It was quiet, no one seemed to be around in the middle of the day.

I put the key into the front door and slowly opened it. "Hello!" I yelled out, just in case someone was here. *What exactly am I looking for here? Where do I even start?* Isobel's room.

I headed down the hallway and took a right, just before the living room. Knowing that Maggie's room was the last one at the end of the hall, I could bypass that for now; I'd start at the beginning of the hallway. I opened the first door to my left.

About halfway open, it hit something. I stuck my head in to determine what I could see—I immediately was repulsed by the smell in this room—ammonia? I saw what blocked the door, it was a box. I pushed a little harder and it moved so I could proceed about a foot into the doorway. That is literally as far as I would be able to move into the space. What I saw was astonishing. Piles of newspapers, stacks of boxes as high as the ceiling, books, a few pieces of furniture stacked on top of each other ... you could not see any of the four walls in this room.

MEOOOWWWRRR ... A very pissed off flash of gray and white flew past me, screaming along the way.

"Holy shi… !!!!" I stammered backward; my heart leapt out of chest. *They have a cat?*

I left the door open only because I wasn't sure what else was trapped in there. I've heard of hoarders before, but I'd never seen it in action. I supposed it was good that it seemed to be contained to this one room. I continued down the hall. *Ugh, what else will I find behind these doors?*

I opened the door across the hall on the right. Isobel's room! It was clean and tidy, thank goodness. My eyes took in the scene as I stepped into the room—light lemon-colored walls and a white wainscoting around the perimeter. There were a few pictures on the walls, mostly floral and they looked to have been painted by Isobel. Her queen size bed had a beautiful summer quilt with sunflowers that accented the walls quite nicely. It wasn't a large room by any means, but with the small white mirrored vanity and a taller yellow dresser in her closet, it was perfect for a twenty-something young woman.

I moved immediately to a white nightstand next to her bed and opened the drawer. There were several candy wrappers, some Chapstick, and a religious pamphlet. Striking out there, I went over to the vanity and opened the long center drawer. There was a silver brush and comb. A few make-up items: blush, eye-shadow, and lipstick, all in shades of pink, along with a few application brushes. I swept my hand farther back in the drawer where I couldn't see after it was pulled out as far out as it would go—a few hair ties, but nothing significant. It struck me how little Isobel had in the way of possessions. *Did she take everything 'camping' with her?*

Opening her closet doors wide, I went through each one of her dresser drawers. There was still a significant amount of clothing left behind in the drawers as well as hanging on the rod that extended the entire length of the closet. But, I didn't find anything that would help me understand what was going on in this household. To look at it all, one would find this normal for a young woman's bedroom. Reaching high up onto the shelf above the clothing rod, I ran my hand along to see if there was anything there to find. Nothing.

I started to feel strange being in someone else's home uninvited. *What if John comes home?* However, I could not help myself; I need to find *something* that explained Isobel's disappearance and helped this investigation. *Let's see what's in Maggie's room.*

My heart dropped again when I walked in there and saw her disheveled bed where the paramedics had removed her. I stood there for a moment, scanning the whole room. It wasn't horribly messy—considering the condition of the first room I saw—but, it also didn't give that warm and fuzzy feeling, like it's a room you'd want to curl up in and sleep for the night. For one, it was dank and dark. I went straight to the window and opened the black-out curtains, letting in the bright sunshine. Yep, that's when I could see all the dust on every surface.

I opened her nightstand drawer and immediately found a cellphone. It was dead, but the charger was there too so I plugged it in to see what I could discover. As it charged, I sifted through tissues, more pill bottles, papers, magazines, and basically just a bunch of crap. I moved over to her dresser and rifled through there too. *What am I looking for? A laptop or tablet would be nice, wouldn't it?*

I didn't find anything except for the phone. When I went back to the window to pull the curtains closed, I could see that it looked out on a detached garage. Hmm, this wasn't the garage I'd seen from the front of the house—it was behind the house. *Ok, let's go check that out, Libby.* Before I headed out back, I took a look at the phone now that it had a little charge. Again, there was no security code to get in … what's with these Crenshaws, don't they know this is for their protection from people like me?

There were 53 missed calls. Fifty of them were from John—ten voice messages apparently is the capacity before the mailbox is full. And, voila, last name is Bell—John Bell. *Ok, at least I learned one new thing rifling through this house!* I started playing the messages.

One week ago. "Maggie, I've got to stay up in Show Low a little longer, wasn't able to get the job done and it'll take at least another day. Call me when you get the message"

Five days ago. "Sweetie, give me a call. Haven't heard from you and I'll be at least another day."

Later, same day, five days ago. "Ok, did you lose your phone? Why aren't you answering?"

There were several more messages like that left each day, until I got to this one: "My boss gave me several more jobs in this area so I won't be home this week. I'm really sorry if I pissed you off. Must be that—I can't understand why you haven't called me back! I have to work. I don't know what you expect, dammit."

Good … he won't be back any time soon, that takes some pressure off as I continue to snoop. I set the phone down to continue charging and I headed for their back door. As soon as I opened it, the really super pissed off gray furball shot past me in a complete blur and so fast I didn't even truly know where it went. *Maybe it wasn't their cat?*

The door to the detached garage was unlocked. I walked into pitch black. Feeling my way along the wall next to the door entrance, I found a switch and it turned on a single light bulb hanging from the ceiling in the center of the building. Not a lot of light, but it'd do. There was a ton of junk in here, but even this wasn't as bad as *that room*.

I suspected this was John's space and where he must spend a lot of time when he wasn't working. I saw workbenches, tons of tools, a broken-down car with no wheels and the hood up, and there was another door at the far end of the room. Opening that door, I could see it was a bathroom—that seems handy. It was decent size for a garage bathroom, I suppose. It was all tiled flooring, a sink with a cabinet beneath it and a toilet. There was space next to the toilet where, if this were in a house, you'd think there would be a shower/tub combination. There was no plumbing for that though. Instead, there was a dark rug, about the same size of a tub, laying on the floor. Looking closer, I noticed that there was something metallic emerging just beyond the border of that rug. I moved the rug back a bit. *A trapdoor in the floor?*

CHAPTER THIRTEEN

I'm pretty sure I stood there for at least five full minutes wondering what on earth a door was doing in a garage bathroom's floor. It was then that I realized the thoughts going on in my head were similar to when you watch a horror film and you plead with the poor helpless woman, yelling at the TV for her to GET OUT! Yes, all those thoughts were swirling around my brain as I bent down and reached for the handle and attempted to pull the door up. It didn't budge at first. I looked around the whole perimeter of the door to see if there were any clasps, locks, anything preventing it from opening. There was a pair of hook-looking metal pieces that a lock could be attached to, but nothing was currently preventing it from opening. So, I tried again, but this time with more gusto behind it.

The dusty metallic door squealed open and I swear no

less than a hundred spiders scurried everywhere! I jumped back out of the bathroom and danced all around— *Agggghh!! I hate spiders!*

After I squished many bugs, dancing around enough to be certain they weren't on me, I glanced over to a nearby workbench and grabbed a flashlight. Pushing the button, it lit up bright. *Ok, I guess this means I'm proceeding.* I walked back to the dark hole in the ground where all the spiders came out and shined my light into the cavernous depths. There was a wooden staircase leading down about eight feet. *What is this?*

A couple steps down, I found a switch on the wall. I flipped it and a dim light came on down in the hole. I shined the light as I headed down slowly, one step at a time … I pointed it up over my head—clear. Down to the bottom of the creaky steps—clear. I kept going—slowly. When I reached the floor, I breathed a huge sigh of relief, but continued shining bright light into every corner. It looked to be a hallway once I got to the bottom. If my sense of direction was correct, I believe it led back toward the house. Only underground.

At the end the long corridor, I entered a small space, maybe six by six feet at most. There was a twin-sized futon bed. There was also a tiny old TV sitting on a metal table. *What. In. THE. Hell. What was this?!*

I caught a glimpse of something and walked to the bed. It was stripped of coverings and the mattress looked soiled and torn. Between the frame and mattress, something poked out. A book? I reached down while slightly lifting the mattress and out came a bound book. *A journal.* I started flipping through the pages. *Isobel's journal!* Shining the light back on the bed to find a clean spot to sit—I started reading through the journal, losing complete track of time.

I jumped and screamed out loud when my ringtone sounded. The shrill sound in this small, quiet space was enough to give me a heart attack.

"Hello," I answered, breathlessly.

"Hey, Libby!" Greg sounded cheerful.

"Oh my God! You scared me so bad. Hold on, I have to catch my breath." I took in several deep breaths, looked around me to remind myself of my surroundings. I had been so lost in Isobel's writing, I found myself disoriented.

"Hey, what's going on, Libby? Are you ok?"

"Well," *careful, Libby, you are trespassing...* "I stopped by Maggie's to pick up some clothes for her."

"Oh good, is she getting out of the hospital?" he asked.

"Uh, no ... not yet. But, uh ... I thought I'd be prepared for when she does get released."

"So, are you still there then?" he suddenly sounded concerned.

"Yep, and you'll never believe what I found ... Isobel's journal. I think this will explain everything! Oh, and guess what? John's last name is Bell." I realized that I almost sounded giddy.

"Libby, get out!! Get out NOW!" Greg warned.

"What? Why? What's going on, Greg?"

"I don't have time to fully explain right now, but there's a good chance that John is on his way home right now. You need to get out of that house, Libby."

"Well, technically, I'm not in the house anymore ... you see, there's a garage in their back..."

"Get. Out. NOW!" and the line went dead.

Uh. Ok. I started to look around to see if I had set

anything else down. I had the flashlight and the journal, and I placed my phone in my back pocket—good, ready to go. I started down the hallway toward the stairs

Wait. Was that a car I heard? I ran to the stairs.

CHAPTER FOURTEEN

What else can you tell us about John Bell?" JJ asked Rod.

"Is that her mom's boyfriend?" Rod replied in question. JJ nodded, and he continued, "She never talked much about him. She griped endlessly about her mom, though."

"So, to hear your story, Isobel still lived at her moms because of her illnesses? If that's true, how was she going to survive getting out and going camping? Weren't you worried about that?"

"I was. I told her that, too." He leaned in closer, and softened to a near whisper. "I thought the mom was poisoning her and she would get better by getting out of that house."

"What? Did she tell you that?" JJ was visibly shocked.

"No, she never came out and said those words. For

years, her mother had her terrified of the authorities, and taking her away. I don't know how she threatened her, but she was horrified they'd show up—so I think she just toed the line, you know?"

"And that's why you didn't call the police to check on her?"

"What's the use? They'd gone there on multiple occasions and nothing ever happened. Listen, all I know is that we talked often enough that I really came to care for her and I wanted to get her out of there. You know, be her knight in shining armor. I'm just sick that she never showed up and that she is missing. If I'd never suggested camping, maybe she'd still be at home?"

"Did you know that her mom may have tried to kill herself?" JJ tried a surprise tactic.

"Wh-what?" he stammered. Shaking his head, "No, that will devastate Isobel!"

"But, I thought she wanted to get away from her?" JJ asked, confused.

"It's complicated. They were super close, but I think what it boils down to is that she wanted to start living an adult life outside of her mother's control. I know, I know … I have conspiracy theories that more was going on, but really, Isobel never said anything like that."

His attorney turned to JJ and informed him that was enough for today. As soon as JJ walked out of the interrogation room, he noticed he had missed two calls. Greg and Alexis.

"Hey, babe, you called?" Calling the wife back first was just a smart move, he chuckled to himself.

"JJ, I've been worried and was hoping you'd be home today. It's getting late, are you on your way?"

"I'm sorry if you worried, but I decided to talk to

the girl's boyfriend again before I headed back. Oh, and you'll want to meet this Greg that I stayed with last night; Libby found a good one this time around!" After a fairly long, pregnant pause, he realized he hadn't answered the question yet. "I'll be heading home shortly, don't worry, honey."

"Thanks. How are things going? Was that person Greg saw really Isobel?"

"Still not sure. Greg is in Heber with the State Police. Last I heard they were still waiting for a search warrant, but maybe there's an update, I missed a call from him too when I was in with Rod. Called you back first." JJ said, looking at his watch.

"Ok, well we sure miss you. I can't wait to welcome you back…" she ended in her sultriest voice.

"I'm on my way!" JJ perked up at that invitation. "I love you!"

In the car, hands-free, JJ called Greg.

"Hey there, I was beginning to wonder if you'd gone ahead back to town," Greg said when he picked up the phone.

"Just got done with Rod and his attorney. I swear he's talking in circles sometimes … *'Isobel is abused … no, I don't know, that could be in my head'* … I got tired of him about the time his lawyer called it a day. Anyway, what's up?"

"We're still waiting. I swear it takes forever to get judges to do their jobs here! Frustrating."

"Ah, it's the same down in the big city, too. And, you're right, it's super frustrating knowing that someone's life could be at stake, or that a perpetrator could run while we just sit and wait. No wonder some cops go rogue." JJ sighed.

"I'm worried about Libby. Have you or your wife talked

to her?"

"Alexis mentioned going to lunch earlier. I guess they all had fun in the park."

"'They all'?" Greg repeated.

"Oh, Alexis, our son Joshua, and Libby," JJ clarified.

"I talked to her earlier and she was at Maggie's house. Probably snooping, but she said she was getting some clothes for Maggie. Anyway, I tried calling her back because we got cut off. I can't get hold of her. So, if either of you hear anything, let her know I'm concerned."

"Yep, will do. Thanks for letting me stay at your place and hey, we should all try to get together after all this settles down. Come visit us in Mesa anytime."

"Sounds like a plan, man. Safe travels." Greg hung up the phone. With a heaviness still weighing on him, and an ominous feeling that wouldn't retreat, he turned his vehicle around and headed down Hwy 260 … toward Phoenix.

CHAPTER FIFTEEN

What's that? I froze. *An engine. Oh no, he's home.*

Sensing that I might be discovered here, I quietly switched off the light and carefully closed the metal door. The car noise didn't sound close. I don't think it pulled into the garage.

Giving myself time to develop a plan, I listened for a few more seconds and let my eyes adjust to the dark. From afar, there was the sound of a car door being slammed shut. My eyes automatically looked skyward as I heard another door.

SLAM!

I jumped, clinging to the stair railing to prevent myself from falling. My heart nearly exploded from my chest. Sweating and breathing sporadically, I felt lightheaded and dizzy. I reached for my phone. *Shit!* Along with the flashlight, they fell down the staircase. The sound was deafening; I prayed whoever was inside the house didn't hear it. Cautiously, feeling for each step, I slowly made my way to the hallway below. I got down on all fours and started feeling all around, ignoring the thought of all the creepy crawlies.

Click!

Was that the metal door?

Just then, I felt something to my right. *My phone!* I used the flashlight app on the phone to find the flashlight I dropped. I made my way down the hallway. If someone opens that metal door, I want to be hidden.

I found the room again and crouched in a corner. Creaks from the floor above. Footfalls—louder and louder. I was right; this room is below the main house. I tried so hard to be the smallest version of myself, all the while trying to breathe deeply and not pass out.

Fear had me in its firm grasp.

CHAPTER SIXTEEN

Greg was entering Mesa city limits, past the Salt River on the Northeast end of town. He couldn't remember the last time he'd been in the greater Phoenix metro area, but was certain that he'd never spent much time in Mesa. Now that the cell service was strong again, he tried JJ's number.

"Hey JJ! I couldn't wait—Libby still isn't answering her phone and I have a very bad feeling. I'm just pulling into Mesa now. Have you or Alexis heard from her?" he asked holding his breath.

"No. Wow, you made good time. I've only made it back about an hour ago myself."

"We need to figure out where Maggie lives, and I'd appreciate it if you could come with me to find her. Would you be able to do that?"

"Sure, man…whatever you need." JJ sounded much more worried now. "Listen, Alexis is at the spa right now and if you're coming into town on Power Road, you are right near it now. Do you know where it is?"

Greg glanced around to find a street sign. "Looks like I'm coming up on Thomas Road?"

"Ok, great … before the next light, you'll turn right into a shopping center complex. Their building is at the far northwest corner, separate from the rest of the center. Dharma Inspired Day Spa, can't miss it. I'll meet you there in ten minutes." JJ hung up.

* * *

Alexis was putting the next set of sheets into the laundry when she swore she heard … knocking? She headed through the relaxation room and toward the front doors. As she pulled open the frosted door leading into the front reception area, she saw a tall muscular man with a brown crew cut and probably the bluest eyes she had ever seen. His face was smashed right up to the window with his hands cupped over his forehead trying to see in.

She walked up to the glass front windows, "I'm sorry, we're not open!" She yelled through the glass.

"Alexis! I'm Greg! Libby's friend from up north. JJ is meeting me here, can I come in?"

"Oh! Of course!" she was saying as she unlocked and opened the door. "Greg! So happy to meet you!" And she wrapped her arms around his stiffening torso and embraced him tightly.

"Have you heard from Libby?" he quickly asked.

"No, not since our lunch at the park. Why?" the crease

pinched between her eyebrows.

"I'm worried, Alexis. JJ will be here soon and we're going to try and find her. You don't happen to have Maggie's address? I guess she is a patient here?"

"Yes, she's one of our clients, but she's in the hospital. And we don't normally give out our clients' address."

"I understand. Libby was there picking up some of Maggie's clothes the last time I spoke to her. But, I'm fairly sure that John—who I guess is the boyfriend—was headed home from up north…"

"And, you're waiting for a search warrant on her place up in the mountains … wait, is he involved?"

"Well, I'm not entirely sure, or sure *how* … but I am concerned about where Libby is now and whether he found her in his home. She's not answering her phone, it's going straight to voice mail. That's why I left the police to deal with the warrant and I beelined it to the city."

JJ walked in at that moment. After a nice long hug and kiss from Alexis, he shook Greg's hand, "Good to see you again, man. I'm surprised you headed straight down here."

Alexis looked up the address on their computer and wrote it down for the guys.

"You know, Libby lives right around the corner. Should we head over there just to make sure she didn't make it home? Could be that her phone is dead?" She asked them both.

JJ spoke up, "Sounds like a good plan. Can you do that? We'll head straight for Maggie's, but call if you find her at home and we'll turn around. I'm sure if she hasn't been home since midday, Shadow is probably looking to be let out."

"Ok, sure. Let me grab my purse and lock up and I'll

be out of here."

"Where Josh?" JJ added.

"He's playing over at the neighbors—the Coyne's."

They started heading out the door. "Ok, call us if you find Libby at home."

Greg piped up, "I'll drive." And they climbed into his white Tundra.

Pulling up at Libby's, Alexis could tell immediately that she wasn't home. Still, she had a key to the place and went in to find a very excited Shadow in her puppy palace in the living room. She slid open the lock and out bounded the forty-pound ball of energy jumping and squirming everywhere with the excited whimpers and cries.

"Ok, sweet girl ... c'mon, straight outside." She opened the sliding glass door and they both stepped out into the evening air which was still quite balmy. Shadow immediately relieved herself, came back over and jumped up for a quick kiss and then ran circles around the backyard letting out all her energy.

Alexis dialed JJ's phone, "Nope, she's not here. And, yes, Shadow was extremely excited to see me."

"Ok, we just pulled up to Maggie's ... well, we're down the street and across the way a bit. We're watching the place, it's hard to tell if anyone is here. There are a lot of vehicles, but they appear to be out of commission. Wait, Lex ... something's happening, I'll call you back."

He hung up and turned to Greg. "Is that the Bronco?"

"That's it!" he said as they watched it speed off, headed in the opposite direction from where they were.

"Let's go to the house!" JJ said.

"Shouldn't you have your department go after the Bronco?"

"For what? We don't know he's committed a crime and the search warrant in Coconino County doesn't have to do with him … it's Maggie's family's property. Let's go knock on the door and take a gander."

"Ok," Greg said opening his door. "Last time I talked to Libby, she said she found something in a detached garage. Let's go around back … over there." He pointed to a gate to the right side of the house.

CHAPTER SEVENTEEN

I had grown tired, not knowing how long I'd been down in this hole. Listening intently, I kept praying that I wasn't about to learn what this place was used for. I closed my eyes and rested. How many hours have passed? Then, I heard it.

Someone was still in the house. A car door slammed, then the engine revved.

Staying quiet, still sitting on the floor in the dark, I listened for any further movement. After several minutes, I began to breathe a sigh of relief. *I think he's gone?*

Releasing my death grip on the flashlight, I moved my fingers around, trying to get the blood flow going again. I felt up and down on the handle until I found the soft plastic on/off button.

The light pierced my brain and I let out a little yelp

and immediately closed my eyes again. Squinting to see out of the tiniest space between my eyelids, I looked around to acquaint myself with my surroundings. It's so amazing what your mind makes up in the dark. Nothing looked familiar and it wasn't at all as I was imagining during those horrifying minutes. *Hours? I have no idea what time it is or how long I've been in this dungeon.*

Listening for any sound, I started to quietly crawl up the staircase once again. Intent on getting out, I attempted to lift my arm up. It felt like a million pounds. Exhausted from this whole experience, I forced myself to find the strength. Using one hand on the railing to hold steady, I lifted my right arm again. The door was just out of reach. I stood on my tippy-toes and made contact with my fingertips. Pushing as hard as my fingers could, it wouldn't budge. I felt my pulse increase again. *If only I could use both hands!* I knew I'd risk falling though. I felt for my phone in my back pocket. I'll call for help.

Wait, what was that? I swear I heard men yelling. I stayed really still. *Where is that coming from? It sounds far away… can't be in the house.*

I waited, listening carefully and dreading being discovered by the grisly man I knew lived here.

"LIBBY!!!!"

That sounded closer. *Hold on, was that my name? Who knows I'm here?*

I listened more intently.

"LIBBY!!!!" The yelling was closer. *Greg? Is that his voice?*

Terrified, but I took a chance that it wasn't John.

"IN HERE!!!" I jumped up slightly hitting the metal door and trying again to lift it upwards. I just wasn't strong enough to lift it from where I stood on the stairs. "HELP!!! HELP!!! I'M IN HERE!!!" I screamed at the top of my lungs and beat the handle end of the flashlight against the metal—over and over again.

Voices were definitely closer now.

CHAPTER EIGHTEEN

Outside the service door to the garage, Greg excitedly said to JJ. "Listen! Hear that?"

"Clanging?"

"LIBBY!!" Greg screamed. "Hey, man, through this door. C'mon!"

"You know, we're trespassing … we can't break and enter!" JJ replied in all his moralistic wonder.

"You're right. You go back to the car, keep a watch out, and call the police if things go south."

"Uh, what exactly are you going to do?" he asked skeptically.

"Don't worry about that. I'm just looking around for Libby. You go…" Greg was getting impatient. "LIBBY!!!" he yelled out again.

JJ's head turned abruptly toward the garage, "I heard a

woman's voice! Probable cause. Have to save a life ... let's go!" They proceeded through the garage side door.

As they walked into the dark, hot shop, they heard it again, a muffled female voice, "IN HERE!"

Greg whirled around looking in all directions. JJ found a light switch and turned it on. They both took in their surroundings ... workbenches, broken down cars, a bathroom. The clanging was coming from the bathroom!

JJ felt the vibration this time when the clanging started. "What the hell?" he said, looking down at his feet. They both crouched down. "A metal door?"

"LIBBY!!!" Greg yelled out.

"IN HERE!!!!!" Clang, clang, clang.

JJ shouted at the floor, "Libby, it's JJ and Greg ... we're here and we'll get you out. Are you injured? Are you alone?"

"I'm alone and I'm fine. Well, except for the spiders ... I'm not fine with the spiders. Greg is here?"

"Yes, he's been worried about you. Don't panic, we'll get you out. Hold on."

JJ made opening the metal door look easy. As soon as it opened, I crawled out and into Greg's arms.

"I was so worried about you!" Greg said breathlessly. "What on earth were you doing down there? Who put you there?"

"No one put me here, I went down there. It's where I found this!" I said, pulling out Isobel's journal from my waist band.

"You willingly chose to go down in that hole?" His face said it all. Not happy.

"Well, I wouldn't say I 'wanted' to go. But, I was curious as to what was down there ... soooooo, yeah, I suppose it was willingly?" My voice trailed off as I realized the gravity of what I said.

JJ was already down in the secret room taking pictures. So much for super-ethical cop—he hadn't even called this in and he definitely didn't have a warrant.

The time I spent down in the secret room afforded me space to consider what I read in Isobel's diary. I needed to go back into the house; I'm onto something. While Greg's back was turned, I snuck out the garage service door and ran.

After a few minutes and once JJ emerged again, they closed the door down, put the rug back in place, and looked all around. "Where's Libby?" JJ asked Greg.

"She was just right here," he answered, turning in a complete circle as he visually inspected the garage. "Dammit!" They both ran out of the garage.

Libby came around the side of the house, nearly running into them.

"Where did you go?" Greg demanded.

"Wasn't sure if I had locked the front door," she grinned, as he looked at her like he didn't even know what to say next.

It was dark out now, but still quiet in the neighborhood. No one seemed to be the wiser and we made it over to Greg's vehicle undetected.

"Where's your car, Libby?" JJ asked, as Greg started pulling away from the curb.

"Turn right, just up there. I'm on the next block over."

"Ok, I'll drive with you over to the spa. I left my car there and Alexis is at your house. Let's all meet there." JJ said solemnly, still not happy with me—that was clear.

* * *

"Libby?" JJ spoke up several minutes into a silent car trip back to the spa. "What were you doing there?"

"Picking up a change of clothes for Maggie?"

"And did you get her those clothes?"

"Uh, well, I…"

"That's what I thought. Now, again, what were you doing there?"

"Ok, so I probably was there to try and learn about Isobel's disappearance more than anything else … and I learned a lot!"

"Libby! That's breaking and entering! Do you know how much trouble we're all in now?"

"I had a key," I said sheepishly.

"Ok, so maybe not breaking in … but you certainly weren't invited, were you? And just how did you get stuck in that room under the garage?"

"Uh, no, I wasn't invited, but in fairness, Maggie's in a coma and I'm sure eventually I would have been asked to get her a few things, so I took it upon…"

"Libby. *How did you get stuck in that room?*" JJ tried again.

"Someone came home while I was down here. I assumed it was John. So, I closed that door so it wasn't evident I was down there." I still saw the disapproving look. "I know, I shouldn't have been snooping … but no one got hurt"

"And, *why* did you go back to the house after we found you? Why would you do that—who cares if the house is left unlocked?"

"I'm sorry. I had one last thing to check on. You're right, it was probably a dumb idea." I quietly sat back and stared out the window. *I may have found exactly what I needed to explain Isobel's disappearance—it was not a dumb idea.*

Once we pulled up to JJ's car in the parking lot, he

jumped out and I got into the driver's seat. Greg was still following us and we all headed off to my home a couple blocks away.

Walking in the front door, I got accosted first by Shadow and then by Alexis. She gave me a huge squeeze.

"My friend, you gave us all a scare. I'm so grateful you are here now." My senses suddenly were filled with the most wonderful aromas coming from the kitchen.

"Thanks, Lexi. What is that wonderful smell?" I asked, hugging my friend back.

"It was getting late and, once the guys confirmed you were safe and on the way home, I took it upon myself to get some dinner going. Hope you don't mind that I helped myself to your InstaPot? And I hope salmon, vegetables, and a nice Pinot Grigio will be ok for dinner tonight?"

"Perfect." I then turned to Greg and JJ, "I'm sorry for worrying you guys, and thank you so much for finding me! I am beyond grateful."

We filled Alexis in on the day's happenings and enjoyed a delicious meal. Looking around the table, my heart warmed as I saw my dear friends accepting the gorgeous ranger into our fold. *I can't believe he's at my house!*

A phone chimed; it was Greg's. Mouthing *the State Police* just before he said, "Chief—hello!" he walked out to the back patio.

After a minute or so, he hung up and came back inside. "They've got the warrant for the Crenshaw Ranch and they are planning to head over there shortly. I thanked him for the call and let him know I'll head back there in the morning." Greg said, looking my direction for approval and then started backtracking. "Um, I can get a motel close by, right?"

"I have a guest room, don't be silly," I said almost too

quickly, then blushing.

"I don't want to put you out, but thought it might be safer to drive back in the daylight."

"Of course, and it's no problem. You saved my life! I think I can spare a room," I smiled.

Alexis and JJ started to clear the dishes and put them in the dishwasher. I showed Greg the rest of the house and where the guest bed and bathroom was. As I rounded the corner coming back into the living area, Lexi was right there with that approving look that clearly stated I better not screw this one up—he's a keeper! I just smiled; no words were spoken.

I held the wine bottle up, looking at Lexi, "Another glass, my friend?"

"No, we've got to pick up Joshua from the neighbor's and get home. Even though this started out as a bit scary not knowing where you were, we've really enjoyed tonight." She gave me a huge hug and then gathered her purse.

Greg rounded the corner to see them collecting their belongings, "Oh no, leaving so soon?"

"Yeah, we have a five-year-old waiting for us so we best get going," JJ stated. "Really hope we can get together again soon. Let us know when you're in town again or if you need any further help with that case." Shaking hands, JJ brought his left hand over Greg's shoulder and clamped down in that makeshift man-hug way, looking him straight in the eyes.

I hugged JJ and again thanked him for bringing me home safely, and they were off. And, I was alone in my home with a man I had met less than two weeks ago, but I felt safer with him than any that I had dated for years. We poured another glass of wine each, listened to some Joss

Stone, and talked about the day's events until my weary eyes couldn't stay awake any longer.

"I've gotta hit it," I said yawning. "You're not leaving super early tomorrow, are you?"

"Unless I get another call, there's no need to beat it out too early."

"Ok, good. I don't have an appointment until afternoon so that's good. We can at least get breakfast before you head out."

"Excellent. Goodnight, Libby." He sweetly leaned over and kissed my cheek before heading down the hall to the guest room.

I took Shadow outside in the backyard one last time before we hit the sack. Standing there in the still warm air, I realized how fortunate I was. Great friends. Nice gentleman showing an interest in me. Terrific four-legged companion. And yes, I was extremely lucky to *not* be in that dungeon tonight. *Thank God they rescued me and I'm sleeping in the comfort of my own bed tonight!* I shuddered to think what would have happened if they hadn't come.

CHAPTER NINETEEN

The early morning light was peeking through at the edge of my curtains. I stretched out really long, my hands way above my head, almost touching the wall behind me and my toes nearly to the edge at the end of the bed. I heard Shadow stir in her crate with her trademark tail thumping on her covers. Deep breath in, deep breath out. Silently, in my head, I started running through all the things I was grateful for. *Shadow, my home, my business, my bed, these soft warm covers, coffee that is about to be made, thankful for kindness, thankful for my friends ... Alexis, JJ, Greg. GREG!* I totally forgot he was asleep in another room in my home.

I hurried to get up and ran into my bathroom. Quickly, I ran a brush through my shoulder length auburn hair and brushed my teeth. I dressed in a pair of black leggings and light blue razor back tank top, let Shadow out of her crate, and headed toward the kitchen to get the coffee brewing.

Shadow ran around the backyard sniffing all the way along the perimeter. I suppose she smells whatever may have invaded our yard during the night, but she took this job super seriously and never came back in the house until every inch was investigated and she'd done all her business.

"Well, good morning!" Greg said, startling me as I turned toward him.

"You sure are quiet, sneaking up on a girl! Good morning. Coffee?"

"You bet."

"Cream or sugar?" I asked.

"Nah, I just take it black. Thanks." He took a sip and sat down at the kitchen table, watching out the sliding glass door to see Shadow's inspection in full swing.

"You have a beautiful place here, Libby. It's nice you are so close to some wide-open desert, even though your home is part of a larger development," he mused.

"Yeah, I love it here. Of course, I wouldn't turn down a ton of acreage somewhere either. But, it's close to work and, like you said, Shadow and I walk just a block or so from here and there are many desert trails to explore. We walk or run nearly every day."

"I don't have to leave for a couple hours, mind if I join you on your journey today?" he asked.

"Fantastic, let's do it! First, I have to finish one cup of coffee before I do anything," I smiled and took a sip from the steaming mug.

Shadow came bounding in through the open door and jumped up to give Greg a kiss. Then, she came over to where I was standing in the kitchen and plopped down on my foot, staring up at me.

"Ok, I'll get your breakfast, sugar!" I said as I scuffed

up the fur on the top of her head and moved to grab her bowl. Her entire body started to squirm where she nearly bent in half turning in circles over and over again.

"Can't control the excitement at that age, can they?" Greg observed. "Wouldn't it be great if we all woke up with this much energy every single day?"

"Dogs sure don't need coffee to get going, not like we do, huh?" I commented.

After Shadow was fed—which literally took a nano second—we finished our cup of coffee on the back patio while Shadow roamed, then we got her bra and leash and set out for a walk. The morning was cooler than it had been recently, but still in the Phoenix area, May is never *cool*. Greg started to sweat almost immediately.

"It's not like up north, is it? Have to get out super early I suppose?" he asked.

"Yeah, now through October, we have to beat the sunrise or it gets quite uncomfortable. I suppose I'm more used to it now too."

"So, are you going to tell me what was in Isobel's journal?" he asked, changing the subject and throwing me off a bit.

"Oh my goodness! I nearly forgot what a crazy day it was yesterday ... how could I have forgotten?"

"That hole in the ground we found you in was something else. What was it exactly?"

"I'm really creeped out by the fact that there is a secret room under the garage. I can't even imagine what goes on down there. I *don't want* to imagine it." I shivered as I thought about the bed, the spiders everywhere

"So, did John come back to the house then?"

"I don't truly know who it was, but assume so. From

underground I could hear footsteps, almost as though someone was running back and forth. Maybe in a hurry to get in and then out? Not sure because it seemed as though they were there *forever*."

Again, a shiver ran up my spine. "But, Isobel's journal was interesting…"

"How so?" he asked

"It was a bit disjointed, but what I did get out of it is that she was definitely trying to get away from her mother. She mentioned in a few entries about hospital visits. The weird thing is that she didn't think she was sick. She was actually questioning why her mom kept taking her to the hospital." I felt myself picking up the pace as we walked along. Shadow was ahead of us and no one was on the trail. "In another entry, she mentioned that social workers had come out to the house—sounds like they did multiple times. She was angry that no one did anything."

"I wonder if she told them about whatever was going on?" he asked, breathing deeply as we climbed a hill.

"Doesn't sound like it. I mean, Maggie must have some kind of control over her. Their relationship is nothing like I thought it was. To listen to her on my massage table, she talked on and on about how close they were. You'd never know it was the same mother that Isobel was writing about in her diary. But, also, the strangest thing is that there were also many entries where Isobel spoke of their closeness and how much she loved her mother."

"Sounds like an extremely complex set of emotions that young one is dealing with. Wonder why the journal was hidden?" Greg asked.

"That's just it. From what I've read so far, I didn't see any mention of that place. So, is that John's 'man cave' or something? Seems extremely odd if it is ... it's *not* comfortable and why does it need to be hidden? Something is off. Something is not right."

"Well, back to the topic of the hospital visits ... you did say that Isobel was diabetic and had asthma, so maybe it's not strange that she had these medical visits?"

"I thought of that, but *she* didn't believe she was sick. That's weird, right? Also, a couple of the entries I read spoke of stomach ailments ... not specifically blood sugar or breathing problems. I haven't been able to shake the feeling there's more to her disappearance and that's why I went back into Maggie's house last night after you and JJ found me." I waited to see if he was going to get upset. He wasn't, so I continued, "I checked her bathroom medicine cabinet and found many drugs that were prescribed for Isobel. I also suspect some of Maggie's drugs that the EMTs took may have been Isobel's as well—really wish I had checked that at the time."

"All of this is bizarre, in my opinion. And how does it explain her disappearance?"

"I'm not entirely sure, but I feel we're really close to finding out."

We were making our way back toward the housing development now and Shadow's tongue was starting to hang out of her mouth, lower and lower. A phone chimed.

"This is Greg," he answered his phone as we were walking back into the house. "Sure, I'm heading back. Should be there in about two hours. Yep, I'll meet you there. Bye."

"So, no breakfast first?" I asked.

"Looks like they've discovered something and I need to get back up there. Wanna go with me?" his eyebrows jiggled up and down excitedly, hoping I'd say yes.

"I've got a massage this afternoon. I also need to call the hospital and check in on Maggie." I semi-pouted. Of course, I'd love to be in the mountains more than here, but duty called.

"Ok. I'll check in later and let you know the latest developments," he said almost over his shoulder as he made his way down the hallway toward the guest room.

"Want me to give the police Isobel's journal?" he called from down the hallway.

I started walking that direction, "Ummm, can we keep it between the two of us for a little bit longer? I'd really like to read more. I promise I'll turn it over though."

"I won't tell ... just make sure you do it soon," he smiled sheepishly. "Ok, I'm headed out. You don't go snooping where you don't belong—stay safe! And, come see me soon?"

"Thank you again for saving me. I'm never going back there! And, yes, let me check my schedule after today and I'll let you know when I plan to head up to see you." My eyes fell to the floor, then back up to meet his in that awkward way when you really don't want to say goodbye. After a brief second or two, we both moved toward each other and hugged for a long moment. As we moved away, he kissed me on the cheek, said goodbye again, and walked out the front door.

* * *

"This is Libby Madsen. I'm a friend of Margaret Crenshaw and I'm checking in ... how is she doing today?" I asked the sweet young voice answering the phone.

"Oh, please hold and I'll transfer you to that unit." Elevator music started. Barry Manilow? My foot started tapping to *Can't Smile Without You.*

"ICU." A more stern and hurried voice answered at the nurse's station.

I repeated who I was and what I wanted, was put on hold again just in time to hear Barry's last words and it moved on to something by the Carpenters. You'd think they'd get a little more modern music.

"Hi Libby," a familiar nurse's voice sounded. I'd spoken several times to Michelle now so we were becoming accustomed to each other's voices. "I do have news today, I'm happy to report."

"Oh good … go on," I said with enthusiasm.

"Well, there's good news and some not so good news," she proceeded. "We have successfully brought Maggie out of the medically induced coma and she's responding well. That's the good news."

"I'd say that's great news!" I interjected.

"Yes, yes, it is. However, the rest isn't the greatest news." She hesitated, then cautiously asked, "How well do you know Maggie? We've tried and tried to find other family members, but it doesn't appear she has any. I really shouldn't give any information about a patient to someone who is not an immediate family member."

"She's been a friend for several years. I'm going to be honest with you, I'm actually helping her to find her missing daughter right now. She does have immediate family, only we cannot find her and it's possible something bad may have happened to her."

After a really deep breath, she asked if she could call me right back and then hung up.

Pacing the floor, I picked up my phone immediately when it started ringing again. "What's going on Michelle? Now, I'm really starting to worry."

"I'm sorry, Libby. I can get in a lot of trouble for doing this, so I took my break and walked outside. I'm calling you from my cell phone." In a lower tone, she continued, "There is something going on with this family. You said her daughter is *missing*?"

"Yes. Are you questioning all the various hospital visits when Maggie brought Isobel in during her childhood?" I asked.

"Yes! You know about that?"

"I'm learning more about it recently, yes. What can you tell me?" I wanted to know how all these pieces fit together. Nothing seemed to be making sense to me. I thought Maggie was a doting mother. Now that I'd found a dungeon, more prescription drugs than any person should ever have on them, and Isobel's journal entries, I agreed with Michelle—something was definitely not right here!

She proceeded to tell me about Isobel's hospital records. Over a period of fifteen years, she was admitted more than seventy-five times.

"Now, mind you, not all visits were at our hospital, but we've tracked down records from many different hospitals all over the valley. Various different ailments—everything from suspected meningitis, leukemia, stomach cancer, liver failure, kidney infection, to influenza, skin rashes, and breathing issues. The problem was—they never found that she actually had these illnesses, but the mother described symptoms and insisted every time that she *must* have 'X'— whatever she claimed that particular visit. One nurse being particularly concerned, called child protective services. The visits slowed for a bit, but then started back up—and, of course, at different medical facilities. When they reached out to CPS again, they were told they investigated and there was no basis, everything was fine in their household—just an overbearing and worried first-time mom. *Fifteen years* this went on."

"Wow, I'm sitting here stunned," I eventually got the words out after what seemed like forever. My head was spinning. I couldn't figure out what this had to do with Isobel's disappearance. *What did she call it … Munchausen Syndrome By Proxy?* Then, I remembered all those prescription drugs. "Wait, if Isobel never had these various illnesses, how did they get so many of the prescriptions?"

"Honestly, I don't know. My guess is that we've only touched the surface on how many doctors she actually went to. I can tell you, they weren't prescribed from ours, but unfortunately there are also unscrupulous, money-hungry doctors out there who will prescribe anything to anybody. She must have found one of them. Also, it's possible that at some of the other hospitals they prescribed things to help Isobel with her immediate discomfort. Remember that she was sick from *something* when she came in—it wasn't necessarily all the varying diseases that Margaret claimed they were."

"Hmmm, ok. What happens next?" I asked.

"Margaret will be moved to a psychiatric unit this afternoon. That is normal protocol for someone who has attempted suicide—seventy-two hours minimum. We are also recommending more in-depth evaluation considering the history we've seen concerning her daughter. It's our belief that this woman has some severe psychiatric issues that must be dealt with."

"Is there any possibility of me speaking to Maggie?"

"No, I'm afraid not. No visitors. Personally, I recommend we let the professionals deal with this. She is going to be extremely agitated the second she understands that she's being moved to Psych."

"Ok. Will you do me a favor then and put my name down as a contact person they can reach out to? And, if possible, let me know who her doctor will be in that unit. I am still looking for her daughter and I'd really like to be kept informed ... especially, if and when they plan on releasing her."

"I'll do my best, Libby. Once she's out of our unit, I have little control over what happens. Plus, no one can know everything I've told you." She sounded sincere about helping, but my optimism waned considerably.

"Thank you, Michelle. I appreciate you telling me all this and I promise not to rat you out. Take care," I said as I hung up.

CHAPTER TWENTY

I spent the rest of the morning, all the way up until my appointment time, researching on my laptop. Munchausen Syndrome by Proxy (MSBP). I had never heard of this and was stunned by what I learned. The implications were huge, and exactly what the nurse was telling me. They think Maggie has MSBP. How could a mother possibly harm their own child? For *fifteen years*. Medical Child Abuse was actually a thing. I sat there staring at my computer screen completely dumbfounded. I simply could not wrap my head around it.

I closed my laptop and jumped into the shower. As the warm water enveloped by body, I pictured that hole in the garage floor. *Is that where she kept Isobel? Surely not, I met Isobel once and she appeared to be a socially adapted young woman. If she were kept in a dungeon for years, being poisoned, wouldn't she appear sickly and definitely not able to converse with others?* Nothing was making sense to me. After getting dressed, and letting Shadow outside, I gathered my bag of clean sheets, oils, and lotions. The mobile table was already loaded in my car so I got Shadow in her crate with a cookie and then proceeded out the door.

All the way to my appointment, I couldn't shake the eerie feeling of everything I'd learned this morning. *Did Maggie kill Isobel, but reported her missing instead?* Ugh, I just couldn't go there. Hopefully, Greg would call soon and the search of the ranch would reveal finding our missing person safe and sound. I really needed to hold onto all the optimism that I could.

I pulled into Sage's neighborhood, with beautiful views of the Superstition Mountains looming ahead. I would never get tired of this view if I lived out here—so amazing! Driving up to her house, I backed up to her little casita where I could unload my gear easily. This is such an ideal location for a 'house call,' I thought to myself. Most clients are struggling to fit me and my table into their already crowded rooms. Some like the living room, others prefer a bedroom, and I have a client who really enjoys their massage out on their backyard patio.

"Good afternoon, Sage," I said as I was unloading and saw her emerge from her home. "You look so relaxed already! Must be the surroundings. Bet you never get tired of this view," I said admiringly as we both took a moment to honor the huge rock peaks that were turning a beautiful deep orange-red color.

"Never gets old, that's for sure," she replied as she opened the casita door for me.

I got all set up and stepped out of the room while she undressed and got settled on the massage table. The beautiful scent of gardenia was floating out of the diffuser today and there was some lovely soft guitar music playing in the background. She had told me previously that her husband was a guitar player and I recognized this as his unique style. It was very relaxing.

For most of the session, she filled me in on what she'd been up to since I saw her last. I listened in that half-conscious way that I do. I really find myself diving into the muscular structure of a body more than I actually *hear* my clients, but even so, I was able to ascertain that she just finished another painting—a landscape this time. She was planning on traveling over to New Mexico in the coming weeks and she was wondering if I'd found Maggie's daughter.

"Uh, wh- what was that?" I had forgotten that we'd talked about them the last time I was here and I was caught off guard. "Oh yeah, you had told me you knew them from years back. Um, no, we haven't found her. But, Maggie is out of her coma now."

"I still say something is really off about that woman," she mumbled with her head smashed into the headrest.

"Yeah, you were saying something about that last time. Tell me more ... what do you think was going on?"

"Honestly? I fully believed the woman has Munchausen's. Well, by proxy. I believe she was harming her kid and that's why I called CPS. They didn't find any evidence and then Margaret, or her daughter, never came back to the pediatric unit I was in. Just weird though."

I didn't want to get Michelle in trouble by divulging what she told me, but I wanted to understand more about what made Sage believe it was MSBP. "What's Munchausen's? I don't think I've ever heard of that."

"In a nutshell, it's medical child abuse. A parent makes up illnesses the child doesn't have—all for the purpose of seeking attention. They literally get off on everything about the medical system. They love the attention of the doctors, nurses ... learning all the ins and outs of medical ailments and treatments. It's truly a sickness. Did you know that some parents actually start poisoning their child to make them sick so they can be admitted to the hospital?" she asked, all flabbergasted.

"That's crazy, Sage." I acted appalled—I *was* appalled! Yes, exactly as I had read about online too, but this was just too much to fully comprehend.

"Yes. Now don't get me wrong, they don't generally grab the rat poison and start giving it to their kid. No, they use prescription drugs, or in some cases common household items that shouldn't be ingested. But, just enough to make them ill, not die."

"How can anyone know how much is ultimately going to kill? Especially a young child." I questioned, with anger growing within me.

"That's just it, sometimes they don't. It's so sad. I saw the strangest things happen when I was in pediatric nursing—just couldn't do it anymore honestly. The system is broken and we're not always able to identify, or save, all the kids."

"Does this happen that often?"

"More than you'd think."

I helped her turn over to her back and from there, we fell into silence once again. Forty-five more minutes to go—the clock on the wall indicated. I spent quite a bit of time working on her quads and feet. When I got to her arms, I pulled out my percussion tool on her forearms, which were particularly tight this week after so much work on her painting. The tool helps to get a little deeper than my hands and fingers could ever do. I maneuvered the pulsating tool up and down her arm and even up into the shoulder area, then to the left side where I did the same. The last twenty minutes, I worked extensively on her neck, shoulders and pectoral muscles.

"Sage," I whispered quietly. "Your session is over. I'm going to step out while you get dressed. Take your time and let me know when you're ready." I stepped out as she stirred. I wasn't quite sure if she was actually asleep or not. She had gotten so quiet.

Once she emerged from the casita, I started packing up my belongings.

"Thank you so much, Libby," she handed me her credit card and I ran it through the card swipe gadget attached to my phone. "I want to leave a twenty-five percent tip as well."

"Wow, that's generous, Sage … you know you don't need to do that," I said humbly.

"No, Libby. I don't *have* to. I *want* to. You help me so much and I don't even have to leave my house!" she laughed as she grabbed her card and put it back in her pocket. "I really appreciate you and I know it has to be hard right now with the pandemic, and clients possibly cancelling on you."

"Well, thank you. I appreciate you too!" I started loading my car, and then turned back again to Sage. "What would you do, outside of the medical profession, if you knew someone today had Munchausen's by Proxy?"

"I'd immediately call CPS."

"What if the victim is no longer a child?" I asked.

"I'd call the police." She reached out to give me a giant

hug. "I hope you find Isobel."

The question that kept swirling around in my mind—
Was Maggie actually poisoning Isobel to keep her sick?

* * *

On my way back to the spa, I called Greg, but only got his voice mail.

"Hey Greg, just curious on how the search of the ranch was going. Also, you're never going to believe half the stuff I learned today. Call me as soon as you can." A little sad when I hung up, I really wished I was up in the hills with that handsome ranger.

I pulled up to our building. No cars anywhere. Dang, I was hoping to run into Alexis. I dragged all my stuff up to the glass front door, pulled out my key and opened the door. Once I had everything inside, I locked it again and headed to the laundry room. I was finished loading the sheets into the washing machine when I heard my phone inside my purse.

"Well, that didn't take long … how's it going up there?" I asked Greg.

"Good and bad news. The good news is that there is evidence that Isobel was definitely here. The bad news is that she is no longer here. They searched the entire place— no luck."

"What led them to believe she was there?" I inquired.

"For one, another journal—more recent one. And, no, I didn't tell them yet about the one you found in her home."

"Thank you."

"There was also some of her clothing and she left without her purse, so they now have actual identification."

"Ok, so that answers one of my questions—Maggie didn't kill her. At least we know she was alive more recently."

"Whoa! Why would you think Maggie killed her?" he quickly inserted.

"Oh man, I have so much to tell you!" I didn't even know where to start, but I also quickly looked at my appointment calendar to see when my next one was scheduled. "Hey, I got done with my afternoon appointment and I don't have anything scheduled now through the weekend. How about I go home, grab Shadow and our camping gear and we'll come up for a few days?"

"Well, that sounds amazing! Would you consider staying at my house instead? In the guest room, of course," he teased.

"Um, we might be able to make that work. I'm sure it would be more comfortable than the tent." We worked out the details and he gave me his address. I checked my watch, it was 3:30 p.m.

"Ok, I'll text when we leave the house. I imagine it will be between six and seven by the time we're in Heber. See you soon." Suddenly, I was excited ... my heart was fluttering again. I geared up into overdrive to get out of town.

CHAPTER TWENTY-ONE

The large dark wooden door opened and those crystal blue ocean eyes beckoned me inside. Shadow blew past me and instantly made herself at home. Greg swept me up into a giant bear hug.

"I can't believe it was just this morning that I said goodbye and now you are at my doorstep," he said in a soothing quiet voice.

"I couldn't believe that I had two cancellations and my schedule opened up for several days. That was lucky! Well, I mean, I need the money … but I think I needed you … I mean, the mountains even more." Whew, that was close. I nearly divulged that I really missed him and couldn't wait for another hug.

"And the *mountains* missed you, too. C'mon in!" He picked up our bags and Shadow's folding crate and welcomed me inside.

We stepped into the great room. I looked around in amazement—there was all wood flooring with tall ceilings, complete with wood beams that stretched across the expanse of the room. Three giant elk horn chandeliers hung across the and the great room on into the kitchen. There was a huge brown leather sectional sofa positioned in front of an impressive rock fireplace. At either end of the sectional, there were also leather recliners that matched the sofa set. There was a huge maroon colored area rug that covered much of the space.

Beyond the living area was the kitchen and a dining area. Tall knotty-pine cabinets throughout. Stainless steel appliances and beautiful forest green Corian countertops, including an island breakfast bar setup with two tall wooden stools. We continued on and there was a hallway with several doors. He opened the door to the guest room and I was quite impressed by this bachelor's interior decorating abilities. It was modest, simple, and clean; there was a queen size bed with a large leather-padded headboard, the soft fluffy brown and green comforter on the bed had deer and pines trees in a quilt-like pattern. There was a small dresser and, just off to the side, there was an ensuite bathroom attached.

"Wow, I'm impressed! You have a very nice home, Mr. Lawson," I said, still looking around. "Now, where did my dog run off to?"

We both headed back down the hall and found Shadow in the master bedroom snooping around.

"Shadow! You need to stay with me, you snoop."

"She's ok. Let her wander." Greg gave Shadow a rub on the head.

"She is still a pup and although she's done well at home and at work, I'm still leery about new places. I should probably get her outside."

He showed us the way to the back door and we all went outside so Shadow could sniff around and go potty. Looking around, I could see that none of his neighbors were super close. This was technically a neighborhood, but he had five acres so there was good space between homes and lots of pine trees made it feel even more private. He had a really nice, large covered patio that stretched all the way around the perimeter of the home. We ended up walking around the property for a little bit and Shadow ran all over the place.

"I have dinner ready when we're done here. It's in the oven keeping warm," Greg said.

"I wondered what smelled so good in there. What are we having?"

"Lasagna and garlic bread. I have a bottle of red I'll open up too."

"Ah, yep, garlic ... that's what I was smelling. Perfect! And, yes, a glass of wine is just what I need. It's been a super interesting forty-eight hours, hasn't it?" I asked as we were entering the back door again.

"Well, don't expect much. It's Stouffer's frozen and not homemade, but they're usually pretty good," he winked, and proceeded to open the bottle of wine.

"Are there any leads as to where Isobel may have gone after the ranch house?" I asked.

"I haven't heard of next steps. I know they were going through her journal and I'm really hoping it helps lead us to where she is now."

"Do you think she was being held against her will?"

"They didn't find anything that indicated she was bound up if that's what you're asking?" he asked curiously.

"That's good. But, I'm so perplexed by all this. Have you ever heard of Munchausen Syndrome by Proxy?"

"Muchha... what? No. What's that?" He legitimately had never heard the term before.

"Ok, so, I got talking to one of the nurses at the hospital that Maggie is at ... oh, and by the way, she's come out of the coma..."

"What? I would have thought you'd have started with that news," he chided.

"I know, I get ahead of myself..." I took a sip of the wine Greg handed me as he began to pull the lasagna and bread from the oven. "I called the hospital to find out how Maggie is doing. She's awake now. Get this, they are moving her to a psychiatric unit."

Greg glanced over at me while he got a couple plates out of the cabinet. "Is that because they think she tried to commit suicide?"

"Yes, but also, no. The nurse confided in me, and I'm not supposed to tell anyone else, but I'm telling you. They discovered in hospital records some anomalies from previous visits with Isobel. This led to figuring out child protective services have been called several times to this family home. Which, led to figuring out that *many* hospitals and doctors over the years have suspected Munchausen's." I took a second to catch my breath and take another sip of wine.

"What is Munchau..."

"Munchausen by Proxy is literally a caregiver harming their dependent—usually a child, but could also be an elderly parent, I guess. They fabricate or induce illness because of their need for continuous caregiving and they also *love* all the sympathetic attention that the medical community gives them when they have a dependent who is really ill."

"What the h…" Greg stared at me.

"I know!" I exclaimed. "I, still to this moment, cannot wrap my head around this! It's CRAZY!" I grabbed the lasagna and bread and followed Greg to the table where we set our plates and silverware.

"Clearly psychotic," he added. "So, what does this have to do with Maggie and Isobel? They actually think she was harming Isobel?"

My head nodded up and down, my eyes large and agreeing on the psychotic part, as I managed the bite of the hot, cheesy lasagna. *Maybe I should have waited for him to dish himself some.*

"Do you believe in synchronicity?" I asked.

Again, he just stared at me.

"Ok, maybe this … do you believe in coincidence or that nothing is coincidental and everything happens for a reason?" I tried again.

"I can get behind everything happens for a reason," he smiled devilishly, as though he meant something else entirely.

"Ok! Good. *Another* client of mine—the appointment I had this afternoon—used to be a pediatric nurse. She knew Maggie and Isobel!" I continued to tell how Sage asked if I'd seen the news story about the missing girl and her whole connection to mother and daughter. "How ironic is that?"

"I'd say it's a small world after all, especially surrounding the Dharma Inspired Day Spa!" he laughed.

"Yes, indeed. Sage and I talked more during her session today about that syndrome and how sick Maggie must be, which confirmed what the ICU nurse was telling me, too. I had the horrifying thought that Isobel isn't missing at all and perhaps Maggie killed her ... got us all looking for her, and then tried to kill herself too. I am relieved to know the police think she is still alive."

"I'm hoping we'll learn more tomorrow."

We enjoyed the rest of our meal and then moved into the living room with the rest of the bottle of wine and Greg started a fire. *The night couldn't be more perfect.* Shadow curled up by my side, after Greg gave her permission to be on the sofa.

"I could sure get used to this," Greg said almost shyly.

I blushed, continued to pet Shadow, and then looked deep into Greg's eyes, agreeing.

CHAPTER TWENTY-TWO

I smelled the warm aroma of arabica beans before I even thought of opening my eyes. Rolling over, I saw Shadow's eyes staring into mine from inside her crate at the side of the bed. Her tail started thumping. Her butt started wiggling.

"Ok, ok..." I got up and put on some sweat pants and a long-sleeved shirt. "Let's go outside." I opened the bedroom door and did my best to steer her directly outside before she wandered off anywhere else.

We blew past Greg at the breakfast bar, drinking his coffee and flipping over the page of his newspaper, before even saying good morning. Straight outside. She went immediately just off the back patio—*thank goodness we made it outside*. There is something stressful about that when staying in someone else's home. In your own home, if a mess is made, it's not great but it's manageable and you don't have to apologize.

"Whew, she had to go!" I said as we came back inside. "It's chilly out this morning."

"Want some coffee?"

"I do!"

I sat next to him at the breakfast bar and stole a section of the paper.

"Whatcha wanna do today?" he asked.

"Wanna stop by and see Charlie and Julie?"

"Sure, why not. And, before we go, I'll call over to the police station and follow up."

"Sounds like a plan. I'll feed Shadow and maybe we can go get some breakfast while we're out?"

"I love your ideas," he agreed.

* * *

The campground wasn't overcrowded as we drove through. Charlie's truck wasn't at their trailer so we decided to drive on and see if he was cleaning up sites. We made it to the end of the road and there were a few campers, but overall, it was fairly quiet for a Thursday. Greg's phone sounded.

"Good morning, Chief," he answered politely as he pulled to the side of the road. Listening to his side of the call only, I caught, "Ah, ha. Ok. I'm over off of 171 at the moment. Yep. Will do."

"Sounds like our plans are changing?" I asked when he hung up.

"We need to head back to Heber, but not until noon. They are following up on a few leads and might be rounding up some volunteers to help again. Wanna help?"

"Of course!"

"We'll head to the substation about noon and see what they're cooking up. In the meantime, breakfast?"

"Sounds like a plan. Let's stop by the house before we get to the station so we can relieve Shadow from the crate for a bit."

We drove slowly past Charlie and Julie's. Still no truck.

"Wait, Julie's there. Let's pull in." I barely caught the movement, off to the side of their trailer where the shadows from the tall pines fell. We pulled into their campsite.

"Hey," Julie said. She seemed subdued.

"Good morning, Julie!" Greg hollered from the truck window before opening the door and getting out.

"How are you doing?" I asked.

She immediately started to cry. *Uh, oh.* Greg pulled her into his arms and gave her a big giant hug.

"There. There. What could possibly be so wrong this early in the morning?" he asked.

Between sobs, she tried to tell us. "Charlie … left me. No vehicle. Except *that…*" as she pointed to their red side-by-side parked at the far end of the trailer. "Left two days ago. We had an argument."

"Oh, Julie," I said, maneuvering over to offer my sympathy too. "I'm sure he'll be back. I'm so sorry."

"Hey, how about you come with us. We're headed to the Café to get some breakfast. Our treat." Julie looked up to Greg at his suggestion and nodded. "Ok, then, lock up and jump in. Let's go get some grub."

The Café was nearly empty as we moved through to find a table out of the way where we could talk quietly. Once our steaming hot coffee arrived at the table and we placed our food order, we tried to comfort Julie who remained silent.

"The police have a lead on Isobel and feel fairly sure she's alive," I piped up.

"Oh. That's good." Julie took a sip of her coffee and didn't seem all that interested in talking.

"Will you tell us more about what happened before Charlie left?" Greg was cautious, but opened the floor for Julie to get it all out.

"He's been sneakin' off a lot lately. He'll b'gone *hours*. So, I asked him about it. He just went off on me. Telling me it ain't no business of mine. 'Course, he'd been drinkin' and all, but he was 'specially nasty so I wasn't mad when he left. At first." She took another sip of coffee.

"So, no explanation of where he's been going? Maybe fishing?" I asked.

"Well, if he gone fishin', seems he'd say so!" she retorted sharp. "Sorry. Nah, not fishin' when all his gear was in the trailer."

"Where do *you* think he's going?" Greg ventured.

She leaned in and quietly started, "Mary over there at the register in the general store was tellin' her knittin' club that he be sneakin' around with the owner's daughter. Seen them plenty of times. Pretty young blonde thing," she scoffed and started to tear up again. "I mean I know I'm no spring chicken anymore, but…" blowing her nose into a tissue she pulled from her pocket, she looked around the room and got even quieter. "But, we're really 'venturous b'tween the sheets, if ya know what I mean," she winked, then started blubbering again.

"Oh boy. Well, until we know for sure, all this is rumor so let's not get too far ahead of ourselves until all the facts are known." I was really trying to be optimistic and comfort her, but the look that crossed her face said anything but comfort. Her look said I'm an idiot.

Our food arrived and we proceeded quietly to enjoy our meals, each of us lost in our own thoughts. Other than consoling Julie, there really wasn't much more to say. We agreed to stop by the store so Julie could get a few grocery items before we dropped her off back at the campground. We promised to check in with her later.

After stopping off to let Shadow out and exercise her a bit with some fetch, we headed over to the police substation.

With masks on, we climbed up the steps and entered the building. The chief greeted us inside the door. "Greg Lawson. Good to see you."

"Chief. You remember Libby Madsen, right? Friend of the missing girl's family. Libby, Chief of Police, Dale Lawrence," Greg said.

"Yes, of course," he said with a giant friendly smile. Both the chief and I moved to carry out the new-normal 'elbow bump' instead of a handshake. "I've got some news for you guys. Come on in my office." He guided us down the hallway and into a nice corner office toward the back of the building.

"First, can I get you any coffee? Water?" he asked. We both waved off saying we'd already had too much. "Alright. Well, I'm not sure what's going on but this young lady has someone helping her out—hiding her. As I told you on the phone yesterday, we didn't find any evidence at the ranch that she was being held against her will. Problem is, we didn't find anything pointing to *who* is with her."

"Well, we saw that Bronco at the ranch … and we know her mother's boyfriend, John, has a Bronco that looks similar. Did you get the plates run? Anything come up on a John Bell?" Greg asked.

"We took the information you fed to us, but I don't have anything conclusive and we haven't been able to talk to him yet. He's as elusive as I've seen. We're trying though." He turned around and grabbed a paper off his printer just behind him. "This is the latest. One of my deputies took this picture this morning. Seems as though we're actually looking for a white—maybe this is a faded silver—pickup?" He leaned across the desk to show us the photo he enlarged and printed out.

"Ugh, not the best quality photo, is it? Hard to make out the people in the cab," Greg said, squinting and struggling to see. "I take it they didn't get a plate number?"

"Unfortunately, he wasn't in position to get that and only quickly was able to snap a picture at all."

"Greg, doesn't this look like Charlie's Ford pickup?" I asked.

"I was thinking the same thing. It's too shadowy to get great detail on the people, but don't they both appear to have light colored hair? Could be blonde? Both seem slight—not heavy body types." Greg kept turning the paper hoping to get a better perspective. "Ok, so now what?"

The chief explained that this photo was taken in Show Low before the deputy lost them. They suspect the couple either knows someone in the area or may be camping.

"If we can get a team of volunteers to help us canvass the campgrounds, we might be able to make more headway in less time," the chief suggested.

"We're here to help. Just let us know where you'd like

us." Greg and the chief leaned in to look at some maps on the desk. Once they finalized the plan and made copies of the map, we were on our way.

Show Low is roughly thirty minutes from Heber. The drive is scenic through more lush pine tree forests, some wide-open rolling hills where ranches reside, and then on into your typical mountain town. I don't generally find myself visiting this town of roughly eleven thousand people often. Of course, it's come in handy on occasion since they have more businesses here than they do in Heber.

"Mind if I just stop in real quick at this hardware store? I remembered something I've been meaning to pick up … won't be but a second," Greg asked.

"Sure, no problem. I'll stay in the truck." It was a gorgeous day out and I was enjoying gazing around at my surroundings and being lost in my own thoughts. So many things were going through my head. I was still worried about Isobel even though the police seemed to think it was hopeful that she's still alive. Yes, that was great news (if true), but I couldn't help think there is anything but being 'ok' for this young lady. What a life she's had already if half of what I've learned so far is true.

I caught a glimpse of Greg running out of the store heading right toward me. *What?* He jumped into the truck quickly and started it and we peeled out of the parking lot kicking up all kinds of dirt behind us.

"What are we doing?"

"You didn't see Charlie?" he asked, out of breath and looking around harried.

"No, I didn't. Where?" I was looking all around and

then realized we were chasing a white pickup that was about five cars ahead of us in the right lane. "He was in the hardware store?"

"Yep, walking out the exit, you know the one at the other end from where I was walking in? I caught sight of someone his size, looked again, and saw this person get into a white truck. There's someone in the passenger seat too. Let's catch up to him and find out where's he's been."

"He's turning right…" I pointed at the same time we came to a stop at a red light.

"Dangit!" he slammed the steering wheel in frustration.

When the light changed green, we proceeded to where we both thought the truck turned. We could see that this put us onto Hwy 260 again, so we just continued toward Pinetop-Lakeside, looking all around for any white truck. Unfortunately, there were white trucks everywhere. Old ones, new ones, Fords and Chevys, *everywhere*. After several more stop lights, we were seriously losing hope of ever catching up to him.

"Look! Isn't that the ol' beater right there?" I pointed ahead to a truck that was pulling out of a McDonald's drive-thru and waiting to turn onto 260 again.

"Could be." Greg was squinting to see. "Now if the light would change!"

Once the light changed, we sped up as much as we could in the heavy traffic and followed the truck with only a couple cars between us.

"Seems as though they are heading out of this area. Who knows how far they're going? Should we continue or get back to the chief's plan instead?" I asked.

"Oh boy, the other cars are turning. Think he'll recognize us behind him?" Greg was already starting to duck lower as though he could hide while driving.

"I thought we wanted him to see us so we could pull over and talk to him?" I was confused now. *Why are we chasing Charlie?*

"Ok, before we are completely out of Pinetop and back to a two-lane road, I'm going to come up on his right side. Let's see if it's even him before we are blatantly obvious about trying to get his attention."

Greg changed lanes and sped up approaching the white truck. We could now definitely see that two blonde headed people were in the truck. Still, from behind it did look like Charlie's size and stringy hair. Coming up alongside the truck, I casually looked over at the passenger.

Isobel?

CHAPTER TWENTY-THREE

Back off!" I yelled at Greg, startling him.

Slowing down, he looked at me like I just sprouted two heads. "What? What's wrong?"

Before answering, I snapped several photos of their license plate as we were retreating. "That's Isobel in that truck! It is *Charlie and Isobel* in there!" I was so shaken by this that I immediately knew we were in danger if Charlie happened to look over and see us. "He never looked over and we need to make sure he doesn't. Just let a couple more cars get between ... follow from a distance. Where's your phone?"

Greg's face looked concerned, but I could see he was still catching up with my thought process and the instructions I'd shouted at him. He pointed to the center console and I opened it to find his phone. I found the chief's number and hit connect.

After several rings, we heard the chief's booming voice through the truck's speakers. "Hi Greg, are you having a hard time finding that location we discussed?"

"Chief, change of plans. We are following an older white Ford truck through the town of Pinetop-Lakeside. We believe the passenger is Isobel Crenshaw."

"Plate number?" Chief Lawrence asked.

I read from the photo on my phone, "Arizona plate … A—D—N—9—9—3"

"Roger that. Alpha. Delta. Nancy. 9-9-3." He repeated.

"Chief, we are headed on Hwy 260 South out of Pinetop-Lakeside, we are nearing the casino and a fork in the road. Ok, it looks like they are staying on 260; maybe heading to McNary or possibly Greer. Does that make sense with where you thought they may be heading?"

"Just maintain a safe distance, Greg, but keep following; I'm calling in for backup now and we'll catch up to you. Call me back if anything changes."

My heart was racing; this was getting exciting. I couldn't figure out why Charlie had Isobel. *Has he been part of her disappearance all along?* None of this added up to the information I thought I learned over the past few days.

"Looks like you are thinking what I am—how does any of this make sense?" Greg interrupted my thoughts. "What in God's green earth is going on here?" He just shook his head.

"They're turning!" I called out. There was no time for us to make the same maneuver and not be detected. I quickly turned my head around to see the street sign as we passed the street they turned on to. "Cooley Ave." I grabbed my phone and chose the navigation app. "Looks like you can turn next on McGaffy Ave. and we can get back to Cooley from there."

Greg followed my directions and after turning off of 260, we turned left again on Fir St., then a right on Cooley Ave. No white truck in sight yet. We proceeded to the end of the street where it veered right and turned into Oak St. As we rounded the corner, we saw what appeared to be a church on our right.

"There they are!" I said excitedly, but then realized they were not alone. "Keep driving—past this entrance. Go slow. Oh shit! There's the Bronco!"

Over at the far side of the first red-brick church building, the white pickup was visible. Charlie was getting out of the truck. The passenger door opened. *I know I saw the Bronco, but where is it now?*

"There's another entrance just down there." I pointed and Greg was already getting ready to turn. "Pull behind that building over there."

The church property was huge. It was completely deserted, except for the white truck and the Bronco I swear I saw. There were several buildings and, once we pulled off the road, we were on the east side of the main building and not visible from the street or the other structures. Greg turned off the truck and called the chief to report our location.

"Let's walk around the back of this building. I'd like to find out if we can see or hear anything going on over there where I saw the vehicles," I suggested.

"I'm not sure we really want to get involved in this; shouldn't we wait for the police to arrive?"

"What if they get away?" I countered.

I opened the door and started to get out whether Greg followed me or not. He did. We crept along the far wall and circled the building carefully checking all around us to ensure we were not seen.

"Shhh, do you hear that?" I asked. We both stopped and listened for a few seconds. Greg nodded his head and we both listened some more. There were three distinctly different voices. "I'd like to get a view if we can do it safely."

We ventured around the back, or southernmost point, of the building. I peeked around the corner and could clearly see two men and a young woman. One of the men was short, skinny as a rail, and had stringy blonde hair. Even with his back toward me, I definitely knew it was Charlie—no doubt about it. The other man was huge and had long black hair and a scruffy face—mountain man like. Even though I wasn't super close, I'd swear it was John. The blonde young woman was not the volunteer girl we'd seen Charlie with before. It had to be Isobel. None of them seemed to be the wiser that we were there. Greg texted the chief with an update and told them 'no sirens' and to approach the church by taking Pollack Ave. to Oak St.

"I'd think they wouldn't want to be sitting ducks this long?" Greg whispered.

"I was thinking the same thing. What are they doing?"

Just about then, Charlie got back in his truck and started it up. John and Isobel were still loading some bags into the Bronco and pulled something out of an ice chest.

How close are you? Greg texted again.

Turning onto Pollock now.

"Crap, Charlie is pulling out of the parking lot!" I said.

"The police are nearly here. Let's get back to our vehicle." Greg grabbed my arm and pulled me back around the corner of the building and we ran back to Whitey. "There they are!" he said, waving his arms up in the air to get their attention.

The first car pulled up to us and then there were three more SUV's that filed in behind. Quickly, Greg gave them the rundown … the description of the Bronco and the perps and they all headed in separate directions to surround them and block all possible exits. The chief pulled up to us just after the rest of the force had vacated.

"Chief, the white truck left. We're going to go look for it. We believe the real perpetrator is on the other side of this building where your team just headed," Greg informed him. The chief agreed and then we headed out and left the neighborhood the opposite way from where the police action would be occurring.

Speeding east on Oak St. to Pollack Ave., then south to 260 again, we assumed Charlie was headed back to Heber/ Forest Lakes area so we turned west. Passing cars left and right, Greg was clearly breaking the law, but diligently hunting down Charlie's truck. I was looking up ahead, left and right. No sign of him.

Miraculously, we made it all the way to US 60 without stopping at one red light. We turned left on US 60 and sped down the main drag through Show Low until we came to the turnoff for 260 again, which would connect us back east toward Heber.

"You don't think he went anywhere else here, do you? Think we should continue toward Heber or go back?" Greg was almost frantic.

"Look! He's getting gas. Circle K. To your left!" I shouted.

Greg immediately turned left and into the Circle K and stopped directly in front of Charlie's white truck. We both jumped out.

"Hey guys! What are you doin' here in Show Low?" Charlie jubilantly shouted out to us as we approached.

"Charlie, what exactly are *you* doing here?" Greg said in the sternest voice I'd heard from him yet.

"Hey, hey, hey ... what's goin' on, Greg? Why so serious?" he asked.

"Charlie, we just saw you with Isobel. Don't deny it," I interjected.

"Isobel?" he looked truly perplexed. "The missin' girl?"

"Yes! We saw you back at that church in McNary!!" Greg yelled. "How do you know John and *why* didn't you tell us she was found!"

"Uh, I have no idear what yur talkin' 'bout." He returned the gas nozzle to the pump. "A friend of mine in McNary asked if I'd mind drivin' his friend's niece from Forest Lakes over to McNary. I said yes. Simple as that."

"You didn't recognize Isobel from all the flyers we have been hanging all over the place for the past couple weeks?" I asked him, trying my best to hold my temper.

"Guys, seriously. I did a friend a favor. What's the big deal?"

Talk about brain dead. He just wasn't getting it. I tried a different approach before I throttled the idiot.

"Charlie, let's just sort out any misunderstanding. Can you come with us for a bit?" I asked in the friendliest tone that I could muster.

"Well, uh, I gotta get back to the missus," he stuttered and shifted his stance.

"Cut it, Charlie ... we know you're in dutch with the missus and aren't heading back there any time soon. Hop in and let's go sort all this out."

Thankfully, he willingly climbed into Greg's truck as

though he was going on an adventure with old friends. Greg parked Charlie's old beater for him off to the side of the gas station in a parking space while I talked his ear off.

"So, having problems with Julie, eh?"

"Ah, Libby … I messed up. I did." He hung his head low looking ashamed.

"Tell me about it. How can I help?" I figured it was best to keep him talking. We might learn something, but even if we didn't, at least it was distracting him.

"She jus' don' understand. I was just tryin' to help and I get accused of all kinds of stuff."

"Like what?" I encouraged.

"What is it 'bout the ladies that they yammer on and believe all kinds of gossip?" he asked. "I mean, she was yellin' on at me 'bout seeing me with a girl and all…"

"Were you with a girl?" I interrupted.

"Well, yeah … but it's not what those nosy-bodies are saying." He huffed.

"Are they talking about the same girl you just dropped off in the parking lot at the church?"

"Nah, 'nother one," he twisted uncomfortably in the back seat. Clearly, I hit a nerve.

It was quiet for a little bit and then Greg got back in the car. Charlie, all of a sudden, started confessing all sorts of stuff. Yes, he cheated on Julie (but only a little bit—not what everyone is saying). No, he didn't have any idea Isobel was the young lady he handed over to John.

"How do you know John?" I asked.

"I don't. Jus' met him twenty minutes ago for the first time."

"Ok, we believe you and we'll explain that to the cops when we get there. However, you probably need to be thinking a little harder about what you know and when you knew it because they're going to grill you pretty hard." Greg was looking at Charlie through the rearview mirror trying to make him more comfortable with eye contact as he explained.

"Cops!?" Charlie blurted out, clearly agitated. "You're taking me in?"

"No, we're headed back to John and Isobel. When we get there, you will see that they've detained the two and are waiting for us to arrive." I glanced over at Greg with an inquisitive look; he must have received a text or call from the chief while we were waiting.

"I can't believe you ratted me out!" Charlie yelled, and then grabbed for the door handle and jumped out.

Greg leaped out to grab him, but stumbled and missed.

The little man was fast and ran off toward the gas station. Both of us took off after him.

Breathing heavily as he rounded the far corner of the station, Greg saw Charlie head off for the trees immediately behind the building. He sped up, and I followed.

Just as I thought Greg was going to lose him, Charlie stumbled on a tree root and fell. Greg immediately pounced and held him to the ground.

"Wh, why ... are you running, Charlie?" he asked, trying to catch his breath.

"I don't wanna talk to no cops!"

"If you've done nothing wrong, then you have no worries, my friend." I tried to rationalize with him, but it didn't seem to work. He was frantic.

Greg held him there until he calmed down. "C'mon Charlie, it's time to go. We're not going to have any more trouble with you if I let you up, will we?"

Charlie harrumphed, but conceded and dutifully walked with us back to the vehicle and we headed back to McNary.

My eyes took in the scene as we pulled into the church parking lot. Red and blue lights were flashing everywhere. The Bronco was surrounded and John Bell was handcuffed and face down on the hood of the vehicle with four cops standing guard. Over at the chief's SUV, we saw Isobel handcuffed and sitting uncomfortably in the backseat. Her face was flushed red and it was obvious she was crying. As soon as Greg stopped the car, I jumped out and ran toward her.

"Chief, why is she handcuffed?" I yelled out.

"Libby, slow down there. Stay back," he cautioned.

"But, she was kidnapped! *He's* the only one who needs to be cuffed," I said pointing over to John.

"We'll see about that, but right now all I know is that these two," the chief pointing back and forth between John and Isobel, "put up a good fight with my officers and tried to get away. Therefore, they are invited to come down to the station and answer some questions."

Greg was on his way over with Charlie. One officer quickly moved in to apprehend and shouted, "Greg, back to your vehicle, please. We'll take care of this."

"Hey, hey …" Charlie said with his hands raised. "I'm innocent. Don't know what's goin' on here."

"Yeah, yeah … that's what they all say." This officer was done playing games and got the cuffs on Charlie immediately. Once he was put inside a third cruiser, the chief came over to us as we waited, patiently staying out of the way.

"Chief, I don't really think Charlie had anything to do with this. I think it was a misunderstanding."

"Well, we'll just see about that. At minimum, he transported a reported kidnap victim. Even if that turns out not to be factual, he left a police scene. Let us do our job now, son."

"Yes, understood, sir."

"Would it be ok now if I talk to Isobel?" I really wanted to make sure she was ok.

"Sure, go ahead. Just a minute and then we're pulling out."

I introduced myself to Isobel and let her know we've been looking for her. She was shaken and scared, but she was okay. I let her know I'd be right there for her and would make sure she had a lawyer for her interrogation. I advised that she shouldn't say anything to the police until her lawyer showed up. She didn't say any words to me, but she nodded in agreement, and I sensed there was some relief in the shoulder tension she was carrying.

"I'll be at the station later. They'll get this mess all sorted and I'll be there to pick you up when they release you. Don't worry." I tried to comfort as best as I could.

CHAPTER TWENTY-FOUR

One month later, with the GPS coordinates plugged into my navigation system, I pulled up to a quaint hacienda-style home in a nice neighborhood. Large trees shaded an oversized lot. There were bougainvillea blooming everywhere around the property, along with beautiful cactus blooms, which provided a nice disguise for the mental health facility.

I turned to my passenger, "Are you sure you're ready for this?" I asked.

To my surprise, the young woman appeared relaxed. "Yes, I'm sure," Isobel answered with a smile. We both turned, unbuckled our seatbelts, and got out of the 4-Runner.

I came around to her side, took her hand and looked deep into her blue eyes. "We don't have to do this right now. We can always come back another time." I squeezed her hand, trying to assure her.

"No. I need to do this and now is just as good a time as any," she replied confidently.

We put our masks on, walked up the short walkway, and pressed the call button outside of the large wooden doors to announce ourselves. After verifying that we had an appointment, they buzzed us right in. We waited in the reception area until a young woman, dressed in pink scrubs with little white sheep printed all over, came to retrieve us.

I kept glancing over to Isobel as we walked down the long hallway and through multiple locked doors. She seemed calm. I was nervous. Finally, we arrived outside a set of doors that you could see through. I could see Maggie sitting in a chair looking out a window. It was unclear whether she was aware of our pending arrival. We walked through the door and continued to follow the nurse over to the window, where she tapped Maggie on the shoulder and whispered something in her ear. It took a minute, but slowly, she turned around and locked eyes with her daughter.

Isobel hesitantly walked toward her and I could see Maggie's eyes well up with tears. Stopping short of an arm's reach, I heard Isobel quietly say, "Hello, Mother." The nurse brought a chair to Isobel and she sat down facing her mother—still, she appeared to maintain a safe distance away. Quietly, the nurse and I stepped back a bit further and took seats of our own, letting them have some private conversation time.

I couldn't even imagine what I would do if I were in Isobel's shoes, but what I had witnessed over the past month was a young woman of great strength and character. She was completely unlike the image I had made up in my own head when I started down this journey of finding her. I had invited her into my home since she had nowhere else to turn. At the time, I was unsure if that was the appropriate thing to do. I didn't know this girl at all. However, now having taken the opportunity to get to know her, I can wholeheartedly say that this was the best decision I have ever made. We became fast friends and she completely opened up to me about everything she'd been through all these years. Of course, I've also made sure she receives appropriate psychiatric therapy because my new friend continues to have a lot to overcome.

I continued to watch her—her tears were flowing now; I could tell even though her back was to me. Maggie tried more than once to reach out for her hand and Isobel pulled back and rejected her. It had to be hard to face someone who abused you for your entire life. Again, I couldn't even imagine myself in this same position. I thought I had it difficult dealing with the death of my father at a young age, but this was entirely different and unique to cope with.

Once they were finished with their visit, I turned to look at Maggie. She gave no indication she even recognized me. I'm sure she was on some heavy-duty sedatives to subdue her, but there was a look that passed between us. Was she thanking me for finding her daughter? Maybe she was grateful that I was giving Isobel a place to stay until she could get herself on her feet? I'll never know and honestly, I didn't care what her feelings were, I was just happy that Isobel was safe now.

As we climbed back in the car, she wiped the remaining tears from her face with the tissue she held. "That wasn't as awful as I imagined," she said quietly.

"I don't know how you did it, Isobel." I squeezed her

hand. "You are incredibly strong and remarkably brave."

"I didn't want to, but I know it's an important part of my therapy. Forgiveness." She sniffled.

"I'm shocked that one month later you felt ready to take this huge step. I'm so proud of you and the courage it took to carry through with it. Yes, I think it will go a long way toward your healing."

"Libby, thank you for letting me stay with you. I promise to get a job and be out of your hair soon." She smiled.

"I have no doubt and, of course, you are always welcome in my home. Just promise me that you'll take the time you need for counseling and taking care of yourself. It's going to take time, you know? There's no need to rush it, that's for sure."

"Yep. You'll hold me accountable, I'm sure." I got a huge smile along with her remark.

"Still ok with having my friends over for dinner tomorrow night? Think you're up to it?" I asked.

"Sounds good to me. I'm really looking forward to seeing that ranger again … I can definitely see what attracted you. Those eyes! They are so kind and *beautiful…*" she ribbed me, laughing. I could tell we were going to get along just fine.

CHAPTER TWENTY-FIVE

"My friend, it has been waaay too long!" Alexis grabbed me up into one of her gracious embraces. "I'm so glad we could all get together this evening." She let me go and latched her eyes onto the beautiful blonde standing off to the side of me. "And, this must be Isobel!"

I don't think Isobel even knew how she ended up enveloped in my friend's arms, but that's how Lexi was. Everyone was hug-worthy and she was the best one to deliver that comfort.

"Isobel, this is my husband, JJ, and my son, Joshua!" She introduced each and then we moved into the living area. "Where's Greg?"

"He's out back with Shadow." I shouted from the kitchen as I put the bottle of Sauvignon Blanc on ice. "Thanks for the wine! Shall I pour?"

"You really have to ask?" she laughed. Her smile absolutely lit up the room; I've always admired that about my friend and I saw that Isobel was also entranced by her.

Greg and Shadow came in and greeted everyone and we sat around on the comfortable sofas drinking wine and listening to some soft rock music. Joshua and Shadow went outside to run around the backyard and play.

JJ looked at Isobel and then to me. "I know this might not be the right time, but I'm extremely curious ... are we okay to talk about the events of the past few weeks?" he asked hesitantly.

I deferred to Isobel, looking her way, "Completely up to you."

"I'm fine talking about it. In fact, I think it really helps." She looked confidently at JJ and then bravely told us all the entire story. Some I hadn't even heard yet either.

We sat in wonder as we learned that John Bell was actually trying to help save her, he hadn't abducted her. Once he figured out what Maggie was up to, and understood he couldn't divulge what he knew without harming Isobel even more, he knew he had to get that girl away from her mother. It was actually his suggestion to Isobel that she try to get approval to go camping with friends. Rod—the boyfriend she had met online, but never actually in person, also wanted to help. She had confided in John about Rod and he agreed they'd probably need help so he approved. Between the two of them, they'd save her—that was the plan.

He was convinced that if Isobel went on the camping trip and found happiness outside the home, she might be able to get out for good. After a long period of time, he helped Maggie see that's exactly what a normal twenty-something should be doing and it would be okay. Finally, she gave in and agreed—but *immediately* became panicked the instant the girl was out of her control. It was clear the day they left that it was going to be more difficult than they originally thought.

"Why didn't John call the police?" JJ asked.

Isobel rolled her eyes, "I can't tell you the number of times 'the authorities' came to our home and my mom talked her way right out of it and schmoozed whoever came to interview us. And to be fair, she *was* a doting mother … so she thought, and so she could convince *anyone*. He had already seen what happened after authorities came and went. I'd get locked in the dungeon for days."

"So, it was always going to be a missing person case then … whether you were in Arizona or Arkansas?" Alexis piped up. Isobel had shared that the ultimate plan would be to move out of state, preferably Arkansas where John had family that Maggie didn't know about.

"I planned to write her a letter telling her I wasn't coming home. What was she going to do, call the police?"

"Ah! This is the reason she enlisted my help … and, it's also the reason she got extremely weird after I brought the police into it," I said.

"Oh yeah! John watched her go ballistic after the first time they came to interview her. He knew he had to do something." Isobel's eyes cast downward, sad for the first time this evening.

"We don't have to go any further, sweetie," Alexis' warm soothing voice broke in.

"No, I just wish it could have been any other way. You'd think that being in my twenties it wouldn't be such drama to leave home. But, it was. She was terribly afraid of being found out. As well she should."

I got up to check on dinner in the oven, while she continued the story for the group. We learned that John wanted to calm Maggie down and thought some of the sedatives she had would work so that he could be away from the house to figure out next steps with Isobel.

Once he learned that I was heading to the mountains to go looking for her too, he freaked out and starting increasing Maggie's dosage, trying to keep her tired and at home. It turned out, she was also taking meds to calm her anxiety, and therefore caused the overdose, and all kinds of other problems.

"Okay everyone, our roasted chicken is nice and golden brown. Let's refresh drinks and move this party to the table." I called out.

The vegetables were steamed to perfection in the InstaPot, along with some garlic buttered basmati rice that I placed into a serving bowl. I carved some slices off the chicken and placed the platter of meat in the center of the table. Apparently, we were starving because the only sound I heard now was the clinking of silverware.

Isobel broke our food trance, "Whatever happened to Rod? I heard he was arrested and I feel so guilty for that," she asked Greg.

"Chief Lawrence says he's been released. After John confessed the whole story, there was no reason to continue holding Rod. He had to pay some fines for lesser laws he broke, but he's a free man. I guess you haven't heard from him then?" Her look said everything. No, she had not.

"I'm still shocked I found your phone up on a ridge where we were hiking. How'd you lose your phone? From what you told us, it didn't sound like you left the ranch house during that time." I asked Isobel.

"Oh, I can answer that…" Greg said. "John told the police that he knew the sheep herder, Jurgi, who routinely moved his flock around that region, from ranch to ranch. Jurgi never knew it, but *Juan* happened to slip her phone in one of his packs so that anyone tracing it would believe she was off hiking. They'd see the location movement in the region where she said she'd be. Unfortunately, it didn't quite work out that way and it fell out where we found it."

"I completely forgot about the sheep herder!" He knew all along that John was at the ranch.

Greg's eyes met JJ's before they cast downward. I caught the look between the two. "What? You guys know more. Is it more about the Jurgi … or, Juan?" I asked.

JJ looked around at the whole table. "The police questioned both of them after speaking to your camp hosts. They suspected Jurgi as the one who attacked you that night at the camp."

I always assumed it was the hooded fellow, which we now knew to be Rod. But, honestly, I've already put all that behind me. I knew then that someone was trying to scare me into leaving.

"Did Jurgi admit to doing it?"

He shook his head. "They're still investigating. You can press charges if you'd like."

"I wouldn't be able to identify who did it, so unless he told someone else or ends up confessing, I don't really see the point." I lifted my wine glass and took a sip. "I really want all of this behind me; no, I don't think I'll press charges."

We listened more to Isobel's tales of the immense freedom she experienced at the ranch, even though she was 'hiding out.' Again, I found myself in disbelief over the many things we discovered about this young lady's childhood. It now made more sense; those dreams I had of a hospital setting.

"I just want to say," I stood up with my glass of wine. "I feel very blessed that we have this young lady in our friend family now. Isobel, you will be loved here for however long it is you choose. I hope you will be comfortable and can heal from a lifetime of hurt. We're here for you now." Everyone held up their wine glasses and we all toasted. "To Isobel's healing!" Glasses clinked all the way around the table.

Later that night, I knocked on Isobel's door, hoping she hadn't fallen asleep yet. I found her reading in bed and I crossed the room and sat on her bed.

"Just one more thing I forgot." I reached into the pocket on my robe and pulled out the dainty necklace—a beautiful butterfly and flower sparkled in the light of the lamp. Her eyes got super wide and watery.

"*Where* did you find it?" she asked

I reached over and clasped it around her neck. "I thought you'd be missing it. I got it all cleaned up. Shadow found it in the dirt at the campground."

"My grandmother gave this to me when I was five. I miss her." Suddenly she looked sad. "I was devastated when I thought I'd lost it in the mountains. Thank you for finding it, Libby!"

I had learned that Charlie found the necklace while cleaning up at the sheepherder's camp and thought it would make a nice gift for Julie, if no one claimed it. Why it was there, I have no idea. I figure it had something to do with John and his way of continuing the charade of her disappearance, keeping searchers focused in the wrong area until they were able to escape to Arkansas. It didn't matter now. I was just happy she had it back—it obviously meant a great deal to her. I gave her a big hug and wished her goodnight.

Walking down the hall, I found Greg getting situated on the queen-sized inflatable mattress in the room I called an office. Shadow was 'helping' him and I heard grumbling. I went over and grabbed one end of the blanket he was trying to straighten out and helped lay it flat over the bed.

"I think this evening went well…" he said. "She seems to be adjusting nicely."

"I think so. It can't be easy for her, but anything after what she's experienced has to be easier. Thank you for being here tonight."

"Of course. I wouldn't be anywhere else." He gave me a huge smile and we said our goodnights.

Early the next morning, Greg, Isobel, Shadow and I went on a long hike around Usery Pass. It was overcast and comfortable and we planned to go the entire ten miles on the trail that circles the entire mountain. Isobel ran ahead with Shadow; Greg and I brought up the rear.

"I think you made a great decision asking Isobel to stay with you," Greg said quietly. "You two are perfect for each other, you know."

I looked at him curiously, not fully understanding what he was getting at.

"From the things you've told me about your childhood and losing your father, it just sounds like there is healing to be done for both of you. I can see you helping each other." He smiled, and reached for my hand. "I'm hoping I can be part of the pack, too?"

I laughed, "You are definitely part of our tribe, silly!"

I'm one lucky woman.

Thank you for taking the time to read *Shadows in the Forest*. If you enjoyed it please tell your friends, and I would be so grateful if you would consider posting a review. Word of mouth is an author's best friend, and very much appreciated.

Thank you,

Jennifer Morgan

* * *

**Get a free book from Jennifer—
visit her website to find out how!**

**Watch for the next books in this series,
coming very soon!**
The Christmas Fairy – a holiday novella
Spa Shadows (summer,2022)
Shadowed Treasures (summer, 2022)
Shadow Retreats (fall, 2022)

Let's connect!
Website:jenniferjmorgan.com
Email: jennifer@jenniferjmorgan.com
Facebook: facebook.com/profile.
php?id=100076154359528
Twitter: twitter.com/JenniferJMorga3
BookBub: bookbub.com/profile/433830544
Goodreads: goodreads.com/user/show/148099219-
jennifer-morgan

What's next for Libby and Shadow?

Libby's world is rocked to the core when her business partner Alexis—working late one night—is attacked by an intruder at their spa. JJ shows up in full cop mode, terrified that his wife has barely escaped the serial rapist who's been plaguing the city in recent months. But Lexi isn't convinced. Too many seemingly unrelated incidents occur before they realize a decades-old murder and pact between two then-juvenile delinquents could be tied to everything going on now.

Meanwhile, Libby and Greg are flourishing as a couple although she'd certainly like to put off having him meet her nosey mother Julia and sister Jordan just a little while longer. But a delay is not to be, when Julia reports strange happenings in her elder community—someone's been tapping at her window at night and using her pool without her permission. And who are these young, bicycle-riding, backpack-carrying 'gang' members who are hanging around? At first, Libby questions her mother's claims. Maybe it's early-onset Alzheimer's? But as she and Shadow start following the clues, the danger appears much closer than anyone realizes. Could all these neighborhood incidents be connected?

Don't miss *Spa Shadows,* the second in this acclaimed series!

CPSIA information can be obtained
at www.ICGtesting.com
Printed in the USA
LVHW110723201122
733630LV00024B/412